# NO SLEEP

(A Valerie Law FBI Suspense Thriller —Book Four)

BLAKE PIERCE

# Blake Pierce

Blake Pierce is the USA Today bestselling author of the RILEY PAGE mystery series, which includes seventeen books. Blake Pierce is also the author of the MACKENZIE WHITE mystery series, comprising fourteen books; of the AVERY BLACK mystery series, comprising six books; of the KERI LOCKE mystery series, comprising five books; of the MAKING OF RILEY PAIGE mystery series, comprising six books; of the KATE WISE mystery series, comprising seven books; of the CHLOE FINE psychological suspense mystery, comprising six books; of the JESSE HUNT psychological suspense thriller series, comprising twenty four books; of the AU PAIR psychological suspense thriller series, comprising three books; of the ZOE PRIME mystery series, comprising six books; of the ADELE SHARP mystery series, comprising sixteen books, of the EUROPEAN VOYAGE cozy mystery series, comprising four books; of the new LAURA FROST FBI suspense thriller, comprising nine books (and counting); of the new ELLA DARK FBI suspense thriller, comprising eleven books (and counting); of the A YEAR IN EUROPE cozy mystery series, comprising nine books, of the AVA GOLD mystery series, comprising six books (and counting); of the RACHEL GIFT mystery series, comprising eight books (and counting); of the VALERIE LAW mystery series, comprising nine books (and counting); of the PAIGE KING mystery series, comprising six books (and counting); of the MAY MOORE mystery series, comprising six books (and counting); the CORA SHIELDS mystery series, comprising three books (and counting); and the NICKY LYONS FBI suspense thriller series, comprising three books (and counting).

An avid reader and lifelong fan of the mystery and thriller genres, Blake loves to hear from you, so please feel free to visit www.blakepierceauthor.com to learn more and stay in touch.

NO GRACE (Book #8)
NO ESCAPE (Book #9)

**RACHEL GIFT MYSTERY SERIES**
HER LAST WISH (Book #1)
HER LAST CHANCE (Book #2)
HER LAST HOPE (Book #3)
HER LAST FEAR (Book #4)
HER LAST CHOICE (Book #5)
HER LAST BREATH (Book #6)
HER LAST MISTAKE (Book #7)
HER LAST DESIRE (Book #8)

**AVA GOLD MYSTERY SERIES**
CITY OF PREY (Book #1)
CITY OF FEAR (Book #2)
CITY OF BONES (Book #3)
CITY OF GHOSTS (Book #4)
CITY OF DEATH (Book #5)
CITY OF VICE (Book #6)

**A YEAR IN EUROPE**
A MURDER IN PARIS (Book #1)
DEATH IN FLORENCE (Book #2)
VENGEANCE IN VIENNA (Book #3)
A FATALITY IN SPAIN (Book #4)

**ELLA DARK FBI SUSPENSE THRILLER**
GIRL, ALONE (Book #1)
GIRL, TAKEN (Book #2)
GIRL, HUNTED (Book #3)
GIRL, SILENCED (Book #4)
GIRL, VANISHED (Book 5)
GIRL ERASED (Book #6)
GIRL, FORSAKEN (Book #7)
GIRL, TRAPPED (Book #8)
GIRL, EXPENDABLE (Book #9)
GIRL, ESCAPED (Book #10)
GIRL, HIS (Book #11)

## LAURA FROST FBI SUSPENSE THRILLER
ALREADY GONE (Book #1)
ALREADY SEEN (Book #2)
ALREADY TRAPPED (Book #3)
ALREADY MISSING (Book #4)
ALREADY DEAD (Book #5)
ALREADY TAKEN (Book #6)
ALREADY CHOSEN (Book #7)
ALREADY LOST (Book #8)
ALREADY HIS (Book #9)

## EUROPEAN VOYAGE COZY MYSTERY SERIES
MURDER (AND BAKLAVA) (Book #1)
DEATH (AND APPLE STRUDEL) (Book #2)
CRIME (AND LAGER) (Book #3)
MISFORTUNE (AND GOUDA) (Book #4)
CALAMITY (AND A DANISH) (Book #5)
MAYHEM (AND HERRING) (Book #6)

## ADELE SHARP MYSTERY SERIES
LEFT TO DIE (Book #1)
LEFT TO RUN (Book #2)
LEFT TO HIDE (Book #3)
LEFT TO KILL (Book #4)
LEFT TO MURDER (Book #5)
LEFT TO ENVY (Book #6)
LEFT TO LAPSE (Book #7)
LEFT TO VANISH (Book #8)
LEFT TO HUNT (Book #9)
LEFT TO FEAR (Book #10)
LEFT TO PREY (Book #11)
LEFT TO LURE (Book #12)
LEFT TO CRAVE (Book #13)
LEFT TO LOATHE (Book #14)
LEFT TO HARM (Book #15)
LEFT TO RUIN (Book #16)

## THE AU PAIR SERIES

ALMOST GONE (Book#1)
ALMOST LOST (Book #2)
ALMOST DEAD (Book #3)

**ZOE PRIME MYSTERY SERIES**
FACE OF DEATH (Book#1)
FACE OF MURDER (Book #2)
FACE OF FEAR (Book #3)
FACE OF MADNESS (Book #4)
FACE OF FURY (Book #5)
FACE OF DARKNESS (Book #6)

**A JESSIE HUNT PSYCHOLOGICAL SUSPENSE SERIES**
THE PERFECT WIFE (Book #1)
THE PERFECT BLOCK (Book #2)
THE PERFECT HOUSE (Book #3)
THE PERFECT SMILE (Book #4)
THE PERFECT LIE (Book #5)
THE PERFECT LOOK (Book #6)
THE PERFECT AFFAIR (Book #7)
THE PERFECT ALIBI (Book #8)
THE PERFECT NEIGHBOR (Book #9)
THE PERFECT DISGUISE (Book #10)
THE PERFECT SECRET (Book #11)
THE PERFECT FAÇADE (Book #12)
THE PERFECT IMPRESSION (Book #13)
THE PERFECT DECEIT (Book #14)
THE PERFECT MISTRESS (Book #15)
THE PERFECT IMAGE (Book #16)
THE PERFECT VEIL (Book #17)
THE PERFECT INDISCRETION (Book #18)
THE PERFECT RUMOR (Book #19)
THE PERFECT COUPLE (Book #20)
THE PERFECT MURDER (Book #21)
THE PERFECT HUSBAND (Book #22)
THE PERFECT SCANDAL (Book #23)
THE PERFECT MASK (Book #24)

ONCE DORMANT (Book #14)
ONCE SHUNNED (Book #15)
ONCE MISSED (Book #16)
ONCE CHOSEN (Book #17)

**MACKENZIE WHITE MYSTERY SERIES**
BEFORE HE KILLS (Book #1)
BEFORE HE SEES (Book #2)
BEFORE HE COVETS (Book #3)
BEFORE HE TAKES (Book #4)
BEFORE HE NEEDS (Book #5)
BEFORE HE FEELS (Book #6)
BEFORE HE SINS (Book #7)
BEFORE HE HUNTS (Book #8)
BEFORE HE PREYS (Book #9)
BEFORE HE LONGS (Book #10)
BEFORE HE LAPSES (Book #11)
BEFORE HE ENVIES (Book #12)
BEFORE HE STALKS (Book #13)
BEFORE HE HARMS (Book #14)

**AVERY BLACK MYSTERY SERIES**
CAUSE TO KILL (Book #1)
CAUSE TO RUN (Book #2)
CAUSE TO HIDE (Book #3)
CAUSE TO FEAR (Book #4)
CAUSE TO SAVE (Book #5)
CAUSE TO DREAD (Book #6)

**KERI LOCKE MYSTERY SERIES**
A TRACE OF DEATH (Book #1)
A TRACE OF MURDER (Book #2)
A TRACE OF VICE (Book #3)
A TRACE OF CRIME (Book #4)
A TRACE OF HOPE (Book #5)

# PROLOGUE

The eyes stared at Bill from the darkness and made him wary. They always did in that part of town. He had been homeless for nearly a decade, and he had learned never to let his guard down when they stared.

The alleyway was cast in relative darkness. The eyes of the other people there stared at him as he walked around in search of a place to sleep.

Most of those there were homeless like him, but some were drug dealers, others prostitutes. In that warped back alley in Boston, the good, the bad, and the ugly intermingled.

It was almost impossible to tell them apart.

A drop of oily water dripped from a gutter high up above, making its way through the cool night air and then down the collar of Bill's tattered coat.

"Dammit!" he sneered, looking up and feeling the icy wetness run down his back.

A couple who were arguing over their only cigarette saw it happen and laughed at him.

He hated people laughing at him. No one took him seriously. Not even his fellow strays.

Bill started to think the dark alley wouldn't provide a safe spot to sleep, when he saw something that caught his eye.

It was a woman. She was attractive, but she didn't belong there, Bill knew that much. She was too well dressed, wearing a white coat, blue skirt, with her blonde hair tied up nicely.

*What are you doing here?* he thought, looking at her.

She walked furtively, her eyes darting around as if every inch of the alleyway was filled with danger.

*It might be*, Bill agreed to himself. He knew the dangers. He knew how the shadows could swallow up anyone. Sometimes he felt like fighting back.

The woman walked past Bill and accidentally locked eyes with him. He felt something deep inside. He hadn't been so close to beauty in many years. The woman's perfume reached his nostrils, momentarily overpowering the smell of fetid water and unwashed bodies.

She kept walking further along the alleyway and then turned a corner.

His heart raced as she disappeared from view. Now a thought took hold of him. He wanted to follow. Now his mind was filled with a curiosity that had replaced any need to search for a resting place.

He quickened his pace, his worn shoes splashing through several thin puddles of oily water.

Reaching the corner, he watched the woman disappear down another alleyway.

*That was a mistake*, he thought to himself.

And yet, quickly, he followed.

This alleyway had several people sleeping, wrapped in cardboard boxes. But it was less populated. Up ahead, the white coat of the woman was unmistakable.

As he continued in pursuit, Bill became aware that there were fewer people around him. Eventually, as he moved deeper to the back of the alley, there was only him and the woman.

Up ahead, there was a shard of light that cut across the alley from a window above somewhere. As the woman moved into the light, she stopped and then turned slowly.

She locked eyes with Bill.

He opened his mouth to say, 'It's dangerous down here, Miss,' but the words never left him. Instead, he watched in horror as something lurched forward out of the darkness towards the woman.

She let out an ear piercing scream, but that part of town was always filled with screams. Screams of the poor, the forgotten, the abandoned.

No one paid the scream any heed. No one, except for Bill. He stepped forward, his hand outstretched to help the woman.

A flash of something cold and shiny quickly flicked upward.

An overwhelming sense of shock flowed through Bill's nerves as he watched the knife move effortlessly, flicking up and then sideways.

The woman wasn't screaming anymore.

She stepped backwards, holding her neck. And then, she collapsed into a grimy puddle on the alley floor.

Bill was in shock. But that shock was quickly replaced with fear.

The killer was now staring at him. All Bill could see was two pinpoints of light glaring at him like a piece of meat.

The knife moved in the man's hand, and then he let out a low chuckle.

That laugh froze Bill's blood.

The killer then slipped back into the shadows. Not running. Not fleeing as if in panic, but instead, walking slowly, methodically, his footsteps occasionally sloshing through water on the ground.

Bill stared at his hands. They were covered in blood. He looked down at the ground and the woman he had followed, the woman he had wanted to warn about the shadows, stared open-eyed up at nothingness, the pool of blood beneath her body the only clue that she was ever alive to begin with.

# CHAPTER ONE

Valerie sat in the driver's seat listening to the hum of the engine as the car remained still.

She hadn't decided whether she was going to go inside or not.

The street was brightly lit by the midday sun. The houses stood quietly, nestled away at the end of Wilson Street. The windows stared back at Valerie.

*My dad's in there*, Valerie thought to herself, focusing on number 17.

The address her mother had given her was 17 Sycamore Street. Her mother who was in a psychiatric hospital. Her mother who was so fractured mentally that her words and actions could rarely be counted upon.

And yet the address had checked out. She shook her head and almost laughed.

With all the resources of the FBI at her disposal, all those databases and records had turned up nothing. But one address from her mother had located her dad.

Valerie hadn't seen him since she was young. It was before her mother had a full breakdown. Before her mother's delusions had made her believe she needed to cut the evil out of her own children.

Valerie shuddered at the thought.

Something flickered in the rear view mirror. A chill ran up her spine. For the briefest of moments Valerie had thought someone was in the back seat staring at her. Someone who could reach out and grab her by the neck.

She closed her eyes.

"Get it together, Val," she said.

But she suspected it was getting worse. Though no one had diagnosed her, Valerie was slowly coming to terms with a terrifying theory: that she would end up in a psychiatric ward like her mother and her sister, Suzie.

She felt as though the same illness coursed through her veins. Voices and hallucinations were on the cusp of her awareness at the most difficult times.

4

Valerie's greatest fear bubbled away underneath like the engine ticking over beneath its hood. *I'll end up in a straightjacket.*

She shook the thought and switched the engine off.

Action was the best remedy for her paranoid mind.

Stepping out of the car, the air was still, hanging there as if suspended by the golden sunshine above.

With each step forward, Valerie heard her heels against the concrete. They didn't echo. They just sounded and then died off, absorbed into the pristine suburb.

Number 17 now lay in front of her. It was neither perfect nor neglected. A normal house on a normal street. But inside, Valerie hoped to find answers.

She walked up the small path and then onto the porch. Her heart raced furiously as she readied her hand. She was about to knock on a door that had remained shut to her for two decades.

*Knock, knock.*

Footsteps soon answered, and then the door opened. A man stood there looking through the screen door. They locked eyes, and Valerie was certain that the man gasped slightly in recognition.

"You're not as tall as I remember," Valerie said, almost automatically.

The man opened his mouth but said nothing, as if caught in a well of disbelief.

But Valerie didn't need him to speak to identify himself. She felt it in her soul. She was staring at the face of her father. The same man who had walked out on her and her sister when they were kids.

"Aren't you going to open the screen door for your daughter?" Valerie said, trying to joke.

"I don't know what to say," the man finally replied, his face partly obscured by the netted screen door.

Valerie pulled back the tears. She was overwhelmed by the sound of that voice. It took her back to her childhood instantly. Only in that moment did she realize just how much she had missed it, how she had needed it.

"You're a hard man to get a hold of," Valerie said. "I've been trying to find you for some time. Even had the FBI looking for you."

The man flinched at that. "The… The FBI?"

"Don't worry," she said. "You're not in trouble. I work with the FBI; I'm a profiler. I catch serial killers."

The man sighed and looked down at his feet. He looked behind as if trying to see someone inside the house. He then finally pushed the door open and walked out onto the porch.

In the sunlight, he looked older. But he'd kept the same beard, though now graying And he still had a full head of gray hair, neatly combed to the side.

His skin was wrinkled in places, but not so much that he was unrecognizable from the man who had raised Valerie and Suzie for the first decade of their lives.

He rubbed his brow.

"Do you know which one I am?" Valerie asked, feeling all the hurt of abandonment welling up from within.

"Valerie... My little Val," he said softly. He shook his head again in disbelief. "You've grown into a beautiful woman. But I'd know you a mile away. You were always strong headed."

"When did you change your name?" Valerie asked.

"About the time I left you all," he said. "I had to leave it all behind. Start fresh. I knew a guy who could get me a social security number, IDs, everything. And that was it."

"I can't believe you were less than an hour's drive away, Dad," Valerie said, a tear finally breaking loose and running down her cheek. "How could you be so close and never call?"

"I don't expect you to understand," he said. "But... I did love you and your sister. I couldn't stay because of your mom. She was so ill, and I couldn't get help."

"So you left us with it..." Valerie pulled back the sleeve of her jacket, revealing the scars on her arm. "Well, Mom did this to me eventually, after you left. The cops came. She thought she could cut the evil out of me."

"I know..."

"You know?" Valerie covered up the scars and wiped the tears from her face. "And you didn't come for us?"

"It was too late," he said. "You were in the hands of social services. I figured you and your sister would be better off without either of us. Besides, I was deep into my new life. I could have gone to jail for changing my identity."

Valerie felt a whirling storm of regret, anger, and grief. She wanted to hug him. She wanted to hit him. She wanted to arrest him. She wanted to go for a walk and talk about the good old days. She wanted it all, and that brought a bitter confusion.

6

"How is your sister?" he asked.

"She's getting treatment at a psychiatric facility," Valerie said.

Her dad shook his head and whispered "dammit" under his breath.

"I'm sorry to hear that, Val."

"Sorry doesn't quite cut it," Valerie replied. "Maybe if you'd been brave enough to stick around, she wouldn't have ended up in a place like that."

There was a silence between them. Valerie had a million things she wanted to say, but only one question she truly needed answered.

"Are you my dad?" she asked, bluntly.

He looked shocked. "I'm not sure how to answer that."

"Mom says you're not. So..." Valerie pulled out a small package from her inside coat pocket.

"What's that?" he asked.

"It's a swab. I want a saliva test so I can run your DNA sample. Then I can know either way. We both can."

Again, another silence. Valerie looked in his eyes. He was hesitant. He looked away from her gaze.

"I won't do that," he finally said.

"Why not?" Valerie asked, holding up the small package. "This is the least you can do for me."

"I don't know why your mom told you that," he said, firmly. "She's crazy!"

"Don't call her that!" Valerie's protectiveness kicked in. "At least she stayed around!"

"To do what?" he asked. "To cut you? To twist your sister so badly she ended up in an insane asylum? Yeah... She's winning mother of the year awards left, right, and center."

Valerie pushed the package into her father's hands.

"Take the test!"

"I don't need this," he said. "Just... Just leave me alone."

He turned and closed the door behind him.

"Don't you dare walk away from me!" Valerie yelled, tears now streaming down her face.

She took a deep breath and tried to compose herself. But the pain of it. The rejection, after all those years, was too much.

"I'll find out if you're my dad or not. One way or another!"

But the door remained shut.

She turned and walked back to her car, looking down at the DNA test in her hand. As she got back into her car, she looked around at 17

Sycamore Avenue. He had made a pretty nice life for himself. All at the expense of his daughters. At least, that was how Valerie felt.

Driving off, she wondered why he wouldn't take the test. Was it because he knew what the answer would be? If that answer never came, Valerie knew she'd never be able to rest.

If her father was someone else, she wanted to know. It was the last chance she had at having a normal relationship with someone from her family.

Deep down, Valerie yearned for that like a child who just wanted to be loved.

As the sky above clouded over and the first droplets of rain followed, Valerie wiped the tears from her eyes and said to herself: "I'll find out who my dad is, with or without his help."

Now her mind tried to change to another priority. Her boyfriend Tom had made a big deal about them going to a restaurant that evening.

She didn't know why, but Valerie sensed that something big was on the horizon, and that Tom had a surprise up his sleeve.

# CHAPTER TWO

Valerie stared at the flickering white candle in front of her. The restaurant was a special place. It was where Tom had taken her on their first date.

The decor might have been a little ragged, but the food was good, and the memories were even better. Now, a couple of years later, they were sitting here again. Tom was doing his best to keep the conversation going, but Valerie was still thinking about her dad's DNA test, and the fact that he refused to take it.

"It's been a couple of months since your last big case," Tom said, chomping down on his spaghetti. "I know you've still had to consult on some smaller cases, but I have to say, I've been enjoying all of this free time we've had together."

"Me too," Valerie said, only catching herself half listening.

Thoughts of her family were consuming her, and she bitterly resented that her past was stopping her from enjoying something as simple as a meal with the man she loved.

"Valerie," Tom interrupted. "You're miles away."

Valerie looked up at him and smiled.

"Sorry," she replied. "Just a little distracted."

"Everything okay?"

"Yeah," she lied.

Tom nodded gave her a quick, kind nod as if he didn't quite believe her and then went back to his food.

Valerie could tell by the look in his eyes that he had something on his mind, too.

Valerie took a bite of her food, and fixed her eyes on the candle in front of her.

"Why didn't my dad take the DNA test?" she blurted out.

Tom was taken by surprise. He put down his fork and knife and reached out across the table, taking Valerie's hand gently in his.

"It was the least he could do after abandoning me as a kid," Valerie said.

"I know," Tom replied. "Why don't you try again in a week or so? He might just have been taken off guard. After all, the guilt he must feel after all these years. Then you suddenly appear. His own kid."

Valerie pulled her hand back. "It sounds like you sympathize with him?"

Tom paused for a moment.

"I'd do anything for my kid, biological or not," he said. "So, yes, I would do it, but only because I would want to be a part of my kid's life again. You don't abandon the people you love."

Valerie felt a rush of emotion, a feeling of appreciation for having Tom in her life.

Then, for the briefest of moments, she thought the waiter was standing next to their table. She turned to ask for another glass of wine, but there was no one there.

The dread came back to her. She feared she was starting to hallucinate The family illness beckoned from the shadows.

She looked up at Tom and met his gaze.

"I love you," she said, her eyes filled with tears.

Tom leaned across the table, and kissed her on the forehead. "I love you too, Val," he replied. "It'll be okay."

Valerie reached out for Tom's hand.

"Did you mean that?" she asked.

"What?"

"That you wouldn't abandon someone you love?"

"Of course."

"I hope that's true, Tom," she said, wondering if he'd run a mile if she started to have mental health issues like her sister and mother.

"You doubt, it?" Tom asked, his eyes deep as the ocean.

"I feel like everyone I've ever loved has left me, Tom," she said. "My mom and sis through their illnesses. My dad for God knows what reason. I'm sorry, I shouldn't project that onto you."

"Maybe you just need a little reassurance," Tom said, smiling. "There's a reason I booked this restaurant you know. Our first date... And..." Tom stood up, pulled out a small red velvet box from his pocket, and then knelt down beside Valerie.

Valerie felt a flutter of competing emotions. She felt everyone's eyes on her in the restaurant.

Tom opened the box, revealing a beautiful silver engagement ring with a set of sparking diamonds inlaid upon it.

The diamonds caught the candlelight and shimmered.

"Will you marry me, Val?" Tom asked.

There was a gasp of excitement from a table nearby as someone enjoyed the drama.

Valerie didn't know what to say. She loved Tom dearly, but she feared that her problems would destroy both of them.

But how could she say no and embarrass him in front of everyone? She couldn't do that to the man she loved.

"Yes," she said, smiling.

Tom let out an enthusiastic cheer of happiness. He placed the ring on her finger and kissed her on the lips. The staff and customers nearby clapped.

"Champagne, Waiter! Please!" Tom said, his voice full of excitement.

"I can't believe this," Valerie said, moving the ring on her finger. She wished Tom hadn't put her so publicly on the spot like that. But she didn't want to ruin the moment.

The waiter brought another two glasses of champagne to the table. They toasted each other, and the other patrons of the restaurant raised their glasses in glee.

The smiling faces were sweet. But Valerie knew they were just a taste of things to come. Engagements were one of life's big excuses to make a fuss over people.

Valerie hated any type of fuss being made over her. But Tom's happy expression and jovial smile was enough for her to expose herself to that.

That's why she knew she truly loved him. Because she was willing to do things that she never had before.

When it came time to leave, Tom and Valerie tussled over who would pay the bill.

"You better let her have her way, son," a man said from another table. "That's how it goes." A woman in front of him chastised the man for being so sexist. Valerie assumed she was his wife.

Tom held up his hands and let Valerie at least pay her half.

"I suppose it's all coming from the same place," he said, smiling.

Things were changing. Valerie felt anxious about that. What lay up ahead for them was uncertain, but she didn't want to talk about her worries. She didn't want to put a negative spin on Tom's happiness.

She was tired of negativity, herself. She wanted to be happy. In truth, she yearned for it, but she worried that somehow she was cursed. That life had a way of taking happiness from her at a moment's notice.

No, she wouldn't ruin the flow of a special evening.

Something else did that instead.

Valerie's cellphone rang as they were getting ready to leave the table.

Tom's face became forlorn.

"Hello?" Valerie said.

"Agent Law," the familiar voice of Jackson Weller, her boss, grimly spoke. "We need you to come down to HQ. I know it's late. But we've been assigned a new case, and it's imperative that we get started immediately. This could be the most difficult case we've had so far."

The call ended, and Valerie looked at Tom's disappointed expression.

"I suppose," he said. "If we're going to be married, I need to get used to this, don't I?"

Valerie reached out and touched his hand. "I'm sorry, Tom. But if there's another killer on the loose, I have to do my duty."

"One of the reasons I love you," he said, sighing.

"Come on," she said. "We can share a cab."

They walked out of the restaurant, hand in hand. Two lovers embraced by the showering skies.

"It's raining," Valerie said, pulling her coat around her neck.

"It can't rain all the time, Val," Tom said, kissing her on the cheek.

How Valerie wished she could believe that. But in her life, whether her line of work or family, death and pain surrounded her like a shroud.

And it was calling again.

# CHAPTER THREE

Charlie was digging out one of the flowerbeds in his back yard as the kids buzzed around him. He enjoyed working in his yard when off duty. It was a way to decompress. Ever since his time in the military, before he joined the FBI, Charlie had come to realize how important it was to immerse himself in tasks where he could switch his brain off.

Growing things, nurturing a garden, he could put his problems to the side when doing that. The brutality of his work, chasing down serial killers with Valerie and Will, faded into the back of his mind during days like that.

The sun was beating down from above. Charlie wiped his brow.

"Here, you go," Angela said, handing him an iced glass of lemon water. It was his favorite, especially on hot days.

"You must be after something," Charlie joked, taking a large swig of the cold drink.

"Can't a wife be nice to her husband with no ulterior motive in mind?"

"Of course," Charlie said, finishing the drink and then handing it back to his wife. "But…"

Angela laughed. "You know me too well. Just to remind you that I have a video call with the Elipses board, later."

"Ph.D. talk?" Charlie asked.

"Yes, Charlie. Ph.D. talk."

"We should invite Will Cooper over for dinner one night," Charlie said.

Angela laughed again. "Why? Because we're both Ph.D.s? Different fields, you know."

"Yeah," said Charlie. "But then while you two talk shop, I could sneak off and play some video games."

Angela raised an eyebrow. "Just remember, I have that meeting. So you'll need to take the kids."

"Of course."

Angela walked back into their house. Charlie continued digging, occasionally stopping to look over at his two kids, Richard and Georgina.

Georgina was only 3, and Richard 5. They were Charlie's world. They were running around soaking each other with water guns when suddenly little Georgina ran over to her dad.

"Daddy," she said, pulling at Charlie's leg.

"Yes, Honey?" Charlie replied, looking down at his daughter's beautiful brown eyes.

"Who is that man?" she said, pointing to the corner of Charlie's garage.

The hairs stood up on the back of Charlie's neck. Someone *was* standing by the garage, and then he'd dipped behind it as soon as Charlie had looked over.

Charlie had seen combat in the Middle East, and he'd chased enough violent killers down to know that he had enemies.

His blood ran cold at the thought: One of them had come to his family home.

Charlie didn't take his eyes off the corner of the garage for a second. He grabbed hold of the spade he was using to dig, and said to Georgina: "Honey. Get your brother and get inside. Now."

"Why,                                                                              Daddy?"
"Because Daddy has a surprise for you. Now go." It was a lie, but he didn't have time to explain, and he didn't want to frighten her.

Little Georgina ran over to her brother Richard. "Daddy says he has a surprise! We gotta go inside!"

Richard smiled from ear to ear over to his dad. Charlie smiled back, but his heart was beating fervently in his chest. He had to get his family out of harm's way.

Once the two kids were inside, he gripped the handle of his spade, tightly.

There was no time to grab a gun. If the intruder was armed, then he could lean out from behind the garage and take a shot at any moment.

Charlie pushed forward, ducking down low, and then leaning his back against the garage wall. Slowly, he peered around the corner. He could see the edge of someone. Their shoulder and foot poked out slightly.

Leaning down, Charlie decided to go for distraction. He picked up a stone on the ground and lobbed it over the roof of the garage behind the intruder. He watched as the intruder instinctively turned in response.

That was Charlie's opportunity.

He rushed towards the corner of the garage, raising the spade over his head.

Reaching the corner, the intruder came into view.

Charlie's heart raced. And yet the intruder stood there, smiling at him.

"Is this how you greet your brother?" the intruder said.

Charlie lowered the spade. "Christ alive, Marvin. I could have killed you!"

Marvin looked at the spade in Charlie's hand. "It'll take a lot more than some yard tools to kill Marvin Carlson."

"I could have had a gun!" Charlie said, still angry.

"I'd have dodged the bullets. You never were a great shot."

Charlie dropped the spade and the two men embraced.

It had been a long time since Charlie had seen his brother, Marvin. He loved him, but he also feared what knowing him could do.

Marvin had always been one for getting into trouble, and Charlie was acutely aware that as an FBI agent, he couldn't let his brother's less than ethical business endeavors affect his livelihood.

"What are you doing back here?" Charlie asked.

"I've missed you, brother!" Marvin replied.

"Yeah, yeah. What are you doing back here?" Charlie repeated.

"I came to tell you I'm sorry," Marvin said.

Charlie's felt uncertain about such a statement. He had yearned to see his brother in many ways, but he was anxious that their association could pull him into dangerous places.

"You're sorry?" Charlie repeated.

Marvin nodded. "Yeah. I'm sorry I got involved in that mess with that Fargo gang the last time you bailed me out. I wanted to set things right between us. We've been hiding from each other ever since the last time. I miss you. It's not right two brothers not talking to each other. I've thought about coming to see you many times, but I always got cold feet. Thought you might put me in cuffs." He let out an uncertain laugh.

It had been several years since that incident. One of the only times in Charlie's career where he went rogue, rescuing Marvin from a group of gun runners hell bent on killing him.

"So... what's happening? You're a fugitive now, a drug dealer, a smuggler, or what?" Charlie asked.

"Oh, don't be like that. Just the opposite," Marvin said, holding out a business card. "I've been up to a lot, lately."

Charlie grabbed the card, looking at it. "Marvin Carlson Enterprises... And what illegal activity is this a front for?"

"Oh ye of little faith," Marvin said with a wry smile.

15

Sometimes when Marvin smiled, it felt to Charlie like he was looking in the mirror. A mirror universe where he had gone off the tracks.

"Marvin..." Charlie said, hesitating. "It's great to see you, but you know with my job..."

"Bro, it's nothing illegal. I've put all that behind me. Trust me."

"And there's nothing else you want?"

"Oh my, are you a sight for sore eyes!" Angela said, coming out from the house.

"Angela!" Marvin said, grinning. He rushed past his brother and embraced his sister-in-law. "You still with this old fool?"

"I'm thinking of trading him in for a new model," Angela laughed. "So, what brings you to our neck of the woods, Marvin?"

"I just wanted to see you all," he said. "It's been too long."

"Do you have a place to stay?" Angela asked.

"Angela..." Charlie said under his breath.

"Hush, Charlie," she said. "I know how much you've missed your brother. Whatever fallout you two had, this is your opportunity to put it behind you."

"I can stay in a hotel," Marvin offered. Charlie knew his brother's insincerity when he heard it.

"You'll do no such thing," Angela offered. "We have a spare room you can use, and it would be lovely for the kids to see you."

"How could I refuse?" Marvin said.

Charlie smiled awkwardly. He was both happy and concerned about his brother's presence. But before he could make his feelings truly felt, Charlie's phone came to life.

"The big FBI man got a case?" Marvin asked.

"Don't tell me..." Angela said with a sigh.

Charlie answered the phone.

"Hi, Jackson."

"Hello Agent Carlson," came Jackson's stony voice. "I'm sorry to disrupt your down time, but an urgent case has come across my desk. I've already contacted Valerie, but we'll need your know-how to bring this one in."

"And Will?"

"I'm calling him next," Jackson said. "I know he was away to a psychiatric conference, but it's not too far. And this case is taking us to Boston."

"Boston..." Charlie repeated.

16

"Is that a problem?" asked Jackson.

Charlie looked at his wife. She looked back, clearly frustrated.

"No, no problem. I'll be there right away."

"See you at HQ." Jackson hung up.

"Charlie!" Angela said. "You know I have a meeting and you promised to look after the kids."

"I know," Charlie said. "But this sounds like a difficult case, and I can't leave it all to Val and Will."

"Have no fear, Marvin's here," Marvin said. "I can help out with the kids."

"No…" Charlie said sternly.

"I'll still be in the house," Angela said. "It's a video conference call. I'm sure Marvin is capable of keeping an eye on Georgina and Richard for an hour."

But Angela didn't know. She didn't know about the trouble Marvin had found himself in previously. She didn't know about Charlie's continual need to bail him out of that trouble.

Charlie had kept that from his wife because he didn't want her to think bad of his brother.

That dishonesty, or rather, omission, had now backfired.

Marvin patted Charlie on the back. "It's no sweat, Bro."

What other choice did Charlie have? He grinned practically through gritted teeth, and headed inside to get ready to chase down another murderer.

# CHAPTER FOUR

Valerie sipped her second coffee, feeling the warmth of it run down the back of her throat. She hoped it would help wake her up from a potent cocktail of stress and wine.

The cab journey over to Quantico had been a quiet one, and during it, she had thought about Tom.

*Engaged.* That was a word she had never sought out. Lifelong commitment was something she had avoided like the plague. Part of it was the fear that she would be consumed by her family history and make the person she loved miserable. Another part was that, while she fought for good in her career, happy endings were something she didn't believe in. No matter how much she wanted to, the world seemed blighted by evil.

Given those feelings, Valerie felt Tom had put her in a difficult position in front of all those strangers in the restaurant. She didn't want to embarrass or hurt him, but now that she had said yes, what would happen? The engagement was like a runaway train, heading off the rails to some unknown location.

The cab pulled up outside the looming outline of the Mesmer Building in Quantico, a location Valerie knew too well. A building that always led her to treacherous places as an FBI profiler.

After tipping the driver, she walked into the building, passed security at the front door, and then headed through the lobby.

*If buildings could talk,* she thought to herself. *This place would have plenty of twists and turns to reveal.*

The Mesmer Building was a place that had become her base of operations as part of the Criminal Psychopathy Unit. Tracking down violent serial killers had become her calling in life, and with her partners Charlie and Will, it had been a much needed anchor in her mind. It gave her something to hang on to. A way to do good in the world. A point to focus on when everything else was on shaky ground.

Yes, she thought there was plenty of evil in the world, but she was dedicated to facing it and helping people. Even if she could stop one more murder, it would be worthwhile.

The truth was that she and her partners had saved countless lives. Putting serial killers away was a calling they couldn't resist.

Stepping into an elevator with bright brass doors, she rubbed her forehead, happy the effects of the wine with Tom had now evaporated. She pressed a button. It lit up in response, glowing like a beacon.

The elevator began moving upward.

Looking up, she caught her eyes in the polished glass-mirror interior. It made her feel uncomfortable. She looked sad and worried. Valerie wondered if others would see the same thing when they crossed paths with her.

*There goes a tragic life*, she thought. *There goes a woman undone by her own family.*

How could she be engaged when the illness was inside of her, growing each day, trying to get out?

The elevator seemed to grumble back at her, a mechanism straining somewhere. A tension that could snap. She sympathized

Valerie felt she could only hold the symptoms of her crumbling mind at bay for so long. Eventually, they would seep out into the real world and everyone would know. Tom. Her colleagues. Everyone.

Her world would implode after that. The FBI would fire her for being unstable. Tom would leave when he discovered just how deep her scars ran and how those scars could consume him. Sure, he would try his best, but Valerie knew that everyone had a breaking point.

That was why she had stepped away from her mom and sister until recently. She had to leave for her sanity, and Tom would, too. At least, that was the story Valerie had told herself over and over.

The doors to the elevator shunted open, and as Valerie walked through them, she thought she caught a warped shadowy figure in the glass beside her. A dark shadow following wherever she went.

She turned to look into the elevator.

Empty.

Just another trick from her mind.

"Get it together, Valerie," she whispered to herself. She gave herself a moment and then walked down the corridor until she reached the glass doors of the Criminal Psychopathy Unit.

Those three words were now an ever-present part of her life. It was quickly becoming the foundation. As long as she could do her job, she felt she had a fighting chance against the insanity that beckoned.

Helping people was her calling, and she hoped that, in some way, that calling would repay the favor and save her.

The team was already waiting for her in the briefing room. Jackson stood pristine in a black suit at the end of the room, waiting patiently in front of a touchscreen.

Will and Charlie walked over to Valerie, smiling, and welcomed her.

She noticed something off about Charlie straight away. The way his shoulders were dipping slightly. His eyes not as bright as usual. He was worried about something. This wasn't like him. But Valerie would wait until the right moment to ask him about it.

"It's good to see you, Val," Charlie said. "I hope Tom didn't mind us taking you away from him yet again?"

"Of course not," Valerie lied. There was no reason to tell the others about her squabble with Tom. It was her business, and although she trusted Charlie and Will with her life, she didn't have the energy to pick over her relationship with her friends.

She had a job to do. That was what she wanted to focus on moving forward.

"How have you been?" Will asked from behind his glasses, his kind eyes glistening with academic intelligence as they always did.

"I'm fine," Valerie said. "Honestly, guys."

She walked past her two friends and spoke to Jackson.

"What do we have, Chief?" she asked, getting straight to the point.

Jackson sighed. "I believe we may have the start of another escalation, Agent Law."

"How bad?" Valerie asked.

"Two women are dead in Boston," Jackson said. "Brutally murdered. The killer showed a great deal of precision, and a talent for violence."

"What makes you think the murders are connected?" Valerie remained standing while Will and Charlie sat down behind her.

"Much like the victims of the serial killer at the amusement park you caught, these two victims were the same age," Will expanded. "There are a few other similarities between the deaths as well, including the use of a knife, and I think it's worth checking up on."

"I wouldn't have called you all here," Jackson said, "if I didn't think it were imperative that we get moving on this one. The two victims were murdered only a day apart from each other, in two busy and built up areas. The killer is either a fool or highly confident."

Valerie knew what that meant, and seemingly so did Charlie, as he remarked upon it.

"So you think this is some sort of heightened escalation," Charlie said. "This killer is going to go on some sort of killing spree very quickly."

"It's a possibility," Jackson said. "As you know, most serial killers kill to feed an urge. Once they kill, that urge is diminished for a period. When it comes back, over time, they kill again. The gaps between the murders then shortens as the euphoria wears off like a drug, until the killer goes into some sort of blood rage, unable to fulfill his desires. He then kills over and over again at a quickened pace in a vain attempt to satisfy the horrible urges he has inside. I'm concerned with the speed of escalation here."

"So this one seems to have started pretty quickly already? The gap between kills isn't large?" Charlie asked.

"I wonder if this is just the first two victims we've found out about?" Valerie mused.

"It's possible," Will said. "The killer may not be escalating from the very first kill, but perhaps there are other previous murders he has been involved in and authorities haven't been able to link them together as of yet."

"Or these are the only bodies they've discovered," Charlie said grimly.

Valerie thought back to the Klaus killings in Austria back in the eighties, long before her time as an investigator and FBI profiler.

That killer appeared on the scene murdering two people per day, as if he had headed straight into escalation from the word go. As it turned out, he had already claimed five victims before that time, storing the bodies in a grungy little apartment, making ritualistic altars out of them. They were all homeless people, so their disappearances had tragically gone unnoticed.

"We better get moving, then," Valerie said. "If this killer is already murdering people back to back, we can't delay for one moment. Every hour passed is another opportunity for him to kill. And if these two victims are indeed from the same killer, I highly expect him to kill again very soon."

"Be careful with this one," Jackson said, gravely. "I have a feeling he might be more brazen and dangerous than any killer you've yet met so far."

Valerie looked at Will and Charlie. She could feel the apprehension. Jackson rarely exaggerated. If he thought this killer was so dangerous, it was wise for them to listen to him.

21

Valerie rushed through to her office to gather some things, feeling in her bones that the next step on this case would take her and her team into menacing, unknown territory.

# CHAPTER FIVE

Valerie felt the rumble of the plane beneath her feet as they soared through the sky, crossing from Washington, D.C., over to Boston.

The plane juddered slightly from side to side through some turbulence. This perturbed her, but she didn't like to show it. She'd never been a fan of flying, but it was a fear she could usually keep at bay.

But Valerie could feel deep within that her usual faculties weren't as keen. Her mind was preoccupied with her mother and sister, and the issue of her father refusing a DNA test.

Will and Charlie sat either side of her as the plane continued to rumble through the skies.

Will was deep into an issue of a criminal psychology journal, but looked up intermittently, clearly worried about the flight. Charlie was undisturbed even during the rougher moments of turbulence and rarely budged from reading a Stephen King novel he'd brought with him.

Valerie put her hand in her pocket and started looking for a mint. She pulled out a handful of what was inside of it. Some lint, some change, and… There it was sitting on top of a few dimes: the engagement ring Tom had given her. She'd taken it off earlier. Valerie had persuaded herself it was because she didn't want it to get damaged during work. But deep down she knew there was more to it than that.

She was conflicted about the engagement. She loved Tom, but she worried what would happen if the illness got a hold of her in her head. What would that do to Tom?

She gasped, but that gasp only brought instinctive head turns. She didn't have time to hide it from her friends. Charlie and Will were now both looking at the sparkling diamond ring in her hand.

"That's not what I think it is, is it?" Will asked, enthusiastically. "Are congratulations in order?"

"You're engaged?" Charlie said almost leaping out from the seat next to Valerie.

This was exactly what Valerie had wanted to avoid. She was having difficulty coming to terms with her engagement herself; she wasn't quite ready to share with her friends. And yet, accidentally, she had done just that.

The plane engines rumbled. The place vibrated momentarily, and then a brief interlude of silence passed before Charlie prodded verbally again.

"That sure does look like an engagement ring, Val," he said. "You don't need to tell us if you don't want. But if it is what I think it is, I'm really happy for you. Tom is a great guy."

Sighing, Valerie felt a lack of energy seeping into her bones. She didn't have it in her to put up a front and pretend it was something else. Besides, she hated lying to her friends.

"Yes, it's an engagement ring," she said, finally.

Will leaned over and held Valerie's hand in an almost fatherly way. "I'm so pleased for you both. I'd like to echo what Charlie said, Tom is a great guy, and you make a wonderful couple."

*Yes, Tom is a great guy,* Valerie thought. But how long would it take for her illness to ruin his life, just as it had almost ruined hers by twisting her mother and sister into something unrecognizable

She wondered deep down if she would have been better saying no to the proposal, cutting Tom loose from the pain that she inevitably saw in their future. Days, months, years ahead, tainted by an insidious and progressive mental illness. Countless doctors, psychiatrists, and therapists. Money and time wasted as Tom would watch helplessly as Valerie slowly succumbed to the walls of sanity collapsing all around her.

She could see it all. Her fears realized

The plane bumped again in the turbulence, breaking Valerie's rumination.

"Val, you okay?" Charlie asked.

"Eh... Yes."

Charlie gave Will a subtle look before returning to the conversation.

"So, when did Tom ask you? And how did he do it? I want *all* the gory details," Charlie asked, feigning an exceptionally effeminate woman's voice as a joke.

"Cut it out, Charlie... He asked just before I got the call for this case," Valerie said.

"You seem a little distant about it, Val?" Charlie said. "Are you okay?"

"I will be," Valerie said. "It was just kind of sprung on me. I didn't expect it. Not yet, at least."

"You don't need to do anything you don't want to," Will said, gently. "Personally, I think Tom is very good for you, but you shouldn't do anything that will compromise what you want out of life, Valerie. It's a short time on this little rock. Make the most of it, with the people you care most about."

Valerie always loved Will's support. He always seemed to see things from her perspective. He was biased, but biased in her favor That was something she was very happy to have in her life.

The plane juddered slightly in the turbulence. Will grabbed his armrest and dug his nails into it, automatically.

Valerie noticed that his body had become tense and his face an off color.

"It's okay, Will," she said. "It's just turbulence. Something to do with the air currents in this direction. I've taken this flight a few times to Boston, and it's always a little bumpy."

Will nodded, smiling nervously before patting his brow with a handkerchief from his inside pocket.

"I take it you haven't set a date for the big day?" Charlie asked, bringing the conversation back to Valerie.

"Of course not," she said, smirking at her friend. "Tom only just asked me. If things go well and work out between us, it'll be a long engagement. Don't expect wedding bells any time soon."

"And does Tom know that there will be a wait?" Charlie asked.

Valerie hadn't discussed that with him. She thought for a moment. She imagined what Tom would want out of the engagement. She didn't have to wonder long. What Charlie was getting at was correct. Tom was the kind to dive into a family situation with both hands. He came from a healthy, happy background. His own family wasn't torn apart the way Valerie's was. For him, relationships, domesticity, that was the goal. That was where happiness was to be found.

She knew he could never truly understand what it was like to come from a difficult background. Tom's naivety was both endearing and frustrating at times.

Valerie couldn't be certain that marriage was the right path for her. She worried that the poison that was in her family blood, that ran through her veins, that was a poison that could infect Tom's life, too. The last thing she wanted to do was break the spirit of the man she loved.

When it came down to it, she'd leave Tom to set him free, if she had to.

"What about you, Charlie?" Will asked.

Valerie knew what Will was doing. He was changing the topic. He had clearly sensed Valerie's discomfort. She was glad for the change in tact.

"What do you mean?" Charlie asked, sounding surprised.

Valerie had noticed something a little off in Charlie since they had been briefed back at Quantico. He seemed to be carrying a difficult stress of his own.

It was in his shoulders.

It was in his eyes.

She was hoping to have a moment in private to talk to him about it, but it was clear that Will and Charlie were growing closer than they had been before, as Will wouldn't have been so forward with him in the past. She reckoned it was all the time Charlie had been spending on the shooting range, helping Will learn the basics of firearms, though he still didn't carry his own.

Will was able to ask such a question without a wall going up.

"I hope you don't mind me asking," Will continued. "But I have noticed you've been on edge the last couple of hours. It's not like you."

"I'm fine," Charlie seemed a bit shocked that now he was being asked to divulge what was going on in the back of his mind.

"I believe you, but thousands wouldn't," Will said with a kind smile. He had a way of unlocking people. Helping them open up. It seemed to be working.

"My brother," Charlie said after a moment of hesitancy. He shook his head in frustration.

"Your brother?" Valerie asked. "I never knew you had one."

"Yes, I do," Charlie said. "And he has a less than trustworthy track record. But he's now reappeared on the scene. He's even back in my house staying there with my wife and kids as a guest. Getting up to who knows what mischief."

"Why didn't you mentioned him before?" Valerie said, stunned that Charlie had omitted an entire chapter of his life from her.

"He's not exactly someone you'd be very proud of," Charlie said. "He's got a record."

"The soldier and the robber..." Will said, thoughtfully.

"What's that?" Charlie asked.

"It's an old Eastern European story," Will explained. "It's about two brothers: one is an upstanding citizen who fights for his country, and the other is a thief. This brings them into conflict with each other.

26

The soldier worries about his reputation being dragged into the mud if his brother involves him in things he doesn't wish to be part of. And the thief feels that his brother is ashamed of him, which feeds his own resentment and anger."

"And how does it turn out for them?" Charlie asked.

"The soldier is killed in battle defending his town from a group of bandits. His example inspires his brother to change his ways, and he becomes a soldier himself."

"And the moral of the story is?"

"There are several," Will said. "I can get you the text if you want."

Charlie laughed. "No thanks, it sounds like a riot. I'd rather read something more entertaining." He pointed to the copy of Stephen King's *The Dark Half* in his hand.

"I suppose," Will continued. "If there is a *main* moral to the story, it's that, by the brother, the soldier, never compromising himself, he, through his example, helps his brother change. No one is a lost cause. Take from that what you will."

"I don't know, Will," Charlie said. "I've had to help him out of a few too many scrapes in my time. You'd be shocked if I told you the details."

"We're here if you ever need us," Valerie offered, softly.

"I know," Charlie said. "But I think I can handle my own brother. I've had a lifetime of practice. I'm just a little concerned as I can't keep an eye on him from Boston."

"Angela will keep him in check," Valerie laughed.

"Maybe," said Charlie, looking out the window with a somber expression.

The plane banked slightly, and Will gripped his armrest again.

"It's okay, Will. We're getting ready to land," Valerie said.

"Would all passengers please remain seated and wear their seatbelts; we're going to make our approach into Boston airport," the captain's voice said over a scratchy radio speaker somewhere above.

"See?" Valerie said. "There is nothing to worry about."

Charlie then leaned over. "Of course, most crashes happen during landing," he grinned.

Will shook his head. Then he let out a nervous laugh.

Valerie took a breath and tried to get herself back into a more professional mindset.

Soon they would be touching down, once again on the track of a serial killer, this time roaming the streets of Boston with an appetite for destruction, death, and murder.

It would be a tough case. She could feel it in her soul.

Valerie was just glad that the two men sitting on either side of her were going with her into the darkness.

# CHAPTER SIX

Valerie was surprised by how quiet the crime scene was as they approached. Boston was a bustling city, and yet little attention was being given to the macabre events of the previous day.

Two patrol cars sat at the mouth of an alleyway in the back streets of a rundown part of the city. Police tape ran across the alleyway, and two police officers stood guarding the entrance.

Standing next to them was a man in plain clothes. A pressed suit hung off him like it was a size too big, covered partially by a grubby raincoat. Valerie assumed he was the on-duty detective. The point of contact to solve the case. He certainly fit the bill.

"There's a lot of deprivation in this area. A lot of homeless people," Will mused out loud, a strange discomfort creeping into his voice.

Valerie had noted the deprivation, too. Many of the surrounding buildings were run down, covered in patches of damp, and several businesses out on the busier roads nearby looked to be having closing down sales. Cardboard boxes and occasional blankets could be seen around the streets.

This was a place where the homeless lived.

"Seems like a strange location for a serial killer," Charlie said.

"What do you mean?" Will asked.

"It's a busy place, there are a lot of people around. Going by the sleeping bags and cardboard boxes we've seen in some of the streets around here, there are a lot of homeless people hanging around. A lot of eyes to watch you kill. It must mean this serial killer isn't very clever."

"We shouldn't underestimate him," Valerie said. "Sometimes it's not stupidity, but rather a flourish by the killer. He could be showing what he's capable of: able to sneak into the busiest places, kill our victim, and then disappear into the night without being caught or even identified."

As they approached the opening to the alleyway, the man in plain clothes stepped forward. Valerie could see even more clearly that his clothes were not a high priority to him; they hung off him like they belonged more on a hanger. Valerie observed that he was the kind of man who didn't feel comfortable with the trappings of society. He only wore the suit, most probably, because he had to. Professional tropes, so to speak.

"My name is Hank Monaghan," he said stretching his hand out and shaking Valerie's. He then flashed a detective badge. "I'm here to liaise with you. You need anything from the Boston PD, I'll be your point of contact."

Monaghan was the epitome of world weariness. He had deep lines across his forehead as though he had spent most of his life frowning. He smelled of cigarette smoke. His fingernails were tinged with the yellow of it. To Valerie he felt like he didn't much care about appearances or social traditions. She just hoped there was more substance to him if they were to work together on the case, and that he wasn't as reckless with his police work. She didn't care about how he looked, only that he be reliable.

"It's a pleasure to meet you, Detective Monaghan," Valerie said. "The Criminal Psychopathy Unit at Quantico was contacted because you've had two murder victims, and that they may be the first two of many."

"I hope to God not," he said in a gruff voice. "The way this world is heading, though, it wouldn't surprise me."

"We've dealt with this sort of thing before," Charlie offered. "Hopefully we can assess whether the two victims are really connected. And then, if a serial killer is involved, we can try and track him down by predicting his behaviors."

"Serial killer?" Monaghan said with surprise. "My boss said you were specialists. Is that what you specialize in? Serial killers?"

"We try our best," Will said softly. "We're not here to tread on anyone's feet. We're here to assist. To help. We try to get into the mind of the killer, anticipate his next move, then catch him before he can kill again."

"I never cared much for living inside a killer's head," Monaghan said. "If you three are willing to do that for us, be my guest."

Monaghan turned and nodded to the two standing police officers. They pulled up the yellow police tape, and the four forlorn figures slipped underneath into the shadowy world of the alleyway.

Though the sun was still up, Valerie felt the coldness of the alley. The warming embrace of the sun couldn't reach that part of the city. It was obscured by the taller buildings around it. It was fated to remain a cold place. And yet she noticed, lining the walls, evidence of habitation. Belongings left by the city's homeless.

"I take it the homeless people were moved out of here before they had a chance to grab all their things?" Valerie asked.

Their footsteps sounded on the cold wet ground as they walked further into the alleyway.

"We're not cold hearted bastards," Monaghan said. "These people have very little. We wouldn't separate them from what little they have. But a lot of them ran when they heard the screams and saw the blood. I'm sure if anyone actually saw the body, the last place they'd want to be is around here, belongings or not."

It wasn't long before they reached the scene of the killing. Sitting in the middle of the alley was a chalk outline of a body. The ground was stained all around with congealed blood.

"They moved the body this morning," Monaghan said. "Guess you might find some of these helpful." He pulled out a folded=over collection of papers from one of his raincoat's deep pockets and handed them to Valerie.

The paper had been crumpled, but Valerie wasn't about to chastise the detective. Making enemies so quickly was rarely a wise move on such a case.

She opened the papers up in her hands. They were filled with photographs of the victim and how she was found.

Valerie studied each one. The girl's body was covered in blood.

"At least from these photographs," Valerie said to her colleagues, "it appears that the victim was stabbed twice. One slice to the abdomen, and one across the throat."

Valerie handed the photographs to Charlie and Will to look over.

"That's a pretty precise cut," Charlie said. "We could be looking at someone with weapons training."

"Ex-military?" Valerie asked, knowing that Charlie had much experience with these things, being ex-military himself.

"Maybe, maybe not. But I'd say this individual has practiced that type of slice before unless he got very lucky. Look at the cut, it's not at an angle. It doesn't slide down or tick up. It's just straight across the neck, cutting the jugular. The killer would have to be strong, quick, and have deadly dexterity to do this in the dark."

"I wonder…" Will mused.

"What's on your mind, Will?" Valerie asked.

"What if this is a crime of passion?"

"You mean like the killer knew this woman?" asked Charlie.

Will stood deep in thought for a moment, cleaning his glasses on a small yellow cloth from his pocket before putting them back on his face.

"Look at the way she is dressed," he said. "She would stand out here. She doesn't seem to be a lady of the night. She doesn't seem to be homeless, either. So what was she doing here? Perhaps she was going to meet someone she knew. And if you look at the kill, there are no bloodied footprints. The killer appears to have leaped out of the shadows, cut quickly, and then disappeared. It would have been quick, otherwise he would have been chased off, surely, by the other people in the alley."

"That's pretty speculative," Detective Monaghan said. "We don't exactly know how it went down. So far we've not found any witnesses."

Valerie leaned down, crouching over the chalk line that depicted where the body had laid. Those outlines always saddened her. They highlighted what was missing, a living breathing human being who had been cut down by a murderous impulse. Another life gone before its time.

"Did the victim have any ID on her?" Valerie asked Monaghan.

"No, but hopefully we'll identify her soon enough. She isn't dressed for the homeless scene. Someone will report her missing."

Valerie looked around again at this shadow covered alleyway. The cardboard boxes and tents that lined the walls, were a reminder of the people society had forgotten and tossed onto the garbage pile.

She stood up and looked deeper into those shadows, wondering how long it would be until there was another murder, another figure reaching out from the dark places of the city to cut down an innocent person.

"We need everything you have on the previous murder, Detective Monaghan," she finally said. "I've read the initial report, but I want to make sure we haven't missed anything."

"Yeah, I thought you might say that." He handed Valerie a card. "I'll get everything ready and send it over to you, my off hours number is on that card as well. Not one for the FBI coming down here, but now that you're here, we should help each other as much as possible. Let's catch this maniac."

"Thank you, Detective Monaghan," Valerie said.

He nodded gruffly and then walked back up the alleyway.

"What now?" Will asked.

"We should get some of the local PD to canvass the area," Valerie said. "When there is a murder like this, slap bang in the middle of the homeless community, rumors spread around like wild fire. Most of the time they're just hearsay and conjecture, but sometimes a solid lead can turn up. I just hope we get lucky."

Valerie looked back along the alleyway to where the police officers were standing at the entrance. It was a momentary glance, but her observational skills were keen. Something was wrong. It took her a moment to process what that something was.

She noticed the strange new element across the street beyond the two officers in the distance. A women in raggedy clothes was peeking out from behind a large, parked truck. Valerie couldn't be certain from the distance, but she thought the woman looked as though she was experiencing deep remorse or sadness.

"You two stay here," she whispered to Will and Charlie. "There's a woman watching us from over there, and she doesn't look like she wants to be seen. I don't want to spook her, so you both pretend that you're still busying yourself here with detective work."

"You want me to take out a magnifying glass?" Charlie joked.

"I have a deerstalker somewhere, just to add that dash of authenticity," Will joined in.

"Behave," Valerie said wryly, walking away from them towards the street.

"Be careful," Will urged as she walked.

Valerie made sure to make it look like she was doing something else other than responding to the woman's presence. She walked underneath the police cordon and then headed down the street. Out of the corner of her eye, she saw the woman dart behind one of the parked vehicles so as not to be seen.

*She's afraid*, Valerie thought. *But she knows something.*

Valerie knew she'd see her coming towards her from that angle and run, so some strategy was necessary to head her off at the pass.

Walking down the street, Valerie felt that she was finally far enough along so that she could no longer be seen. She doubled back on the other side of the road, now walking along the sidewalk behind the hiding woman.

Quietly, quickly, Valerie was now close to her target. She could see the woman from behind, peeking out from behind the truck and still looking at the crime scene from afar.

Despite trying to move as silently as possible, Valerie's nearing footsteps soon triggered movement. The women, now one only a few feet away, turned around responding to Valerie's careful steps.

Her face dirtied with the grime of the streets, her hair black and matted down, the woman's eyes darted wildly with panic at the sight of Valerie.

She lurched backwards onto the road and then straight into the road. Cars passed her, but she seemed deft on her feet.

Valerie sprinted after her as fast as she could.

"Stop, FBI!"

She followed relentlessly as the woman disappeared around a corner. Moving directly after her, it was Valerie's turn to avoid traffic. She moved between two parked cars and then zigzagged between a motorbike and a bus on the road. A white van passed inches from her and nearly struck Valerie. At the last second, she darted out of its way, never taking her eyes off the woman in front of her.

It was clear to Valerie that the woman knew the area well, better than she did. She moved across the street, down another, and then into another one of Boston's dark alleys as if heading to a definitive location.

But Valerie was relentless in the chase; she would not give up. She stayed on the trail and headed straight into the maw of the alley. Suddenly, she found herself surrounded by homeless people in their makeshift shelters.

Some were on the ground. Others were standing by a small fire in an old trash can. But they were all looking at her.

Valerie turned around, scanning all those who were there carefully until she saw the woman she had been chasing, standing, sobbing into a man's shoulder.

"You can't kill her here," the man said. "There's too many of us."

Valerie pulled out her badge and showed it to the disheveled man. "I'm with the FBI. There's been enough death around here already. I'm trying to stop it from happening again. I'm trying to protect you."

Valerie and the woman locked eyes.

"It's going to be okay," Valerie said. "I just want to ask a few questions... I saw you looking at us in the alley where the victim had been murdered. You had an expression of someone who had seen something terrible."

"I... I don't know," the women said in a thick accent. Valerie reckoned it was Eastern European.

34

"I swear, I'm not here to hurt you," Valerie said. "I'm not here to arrest you either. The woman who was murdered in the alleyway... I have a feeling you know something about it. Maybe you saw something or heard something about it?"

Valerie noticed the woman's body language. She seemed to be relaxing slightly. She was beginning to realize she wasn't in danger. Trust was building, though slowly.

"I know you may not want to talk to someone in law enforcement," Valerie continued. "But I'm here to protect everyone in this neighborhood. I want to make sure that no one else is killed. If you tell me what you know, it could help me stop another murder from happening. Will you help me?"

The women looked at the man she had embraced. He nodded to her as if agreeing with what Valerie was saying.

The woman studied Valerie for a moment, opened her mouth, and then said: "I know someone who saw what happened. His name is Bill. He saw that poor woman killed."

"Does this Bill have a second name? Do you know it?" Valerie asked.

"No," the woman replied. "But you might find him sleeping around here. He's always hanging about. He's a good guy. Helps people when he can. He helped me fit in when I first got here.

"I saw him run out of the alley when the screaming started last night. He bumped into me. He... He had blood on his hands. But he told me it was because he was standing next to the victim when she was killed. Bill is a nice man. I believe him. How do you say... He wouldn't harm a fly."

Valerie had heard that many times before from people. Just because they thought he was harmless, it didn't mean he was, in reality. She'd need to carefully consider him as either a witness or potential suspect.

"Why were you hiding behind the truck watching the investigation?" Valerie asked.

The woman hesitated. "My stuff... I live down there. I have some things that are sentimental. It's all I have. Now the police will take it away."

Valerie cast her mind back to the abandoned cardboard boxes, tents, and belongings in and around the murder scene.

"That won't happen. I won't let it. What's your name?" Valerie asked. "Just so I can contact you again and make sure you get your things."

"Marta Vargova," she said timidly. "I'll be staying down this alley with Fred here for a bit. But there is a drop-in center just around the corner. They give me clothes and medicine and food. If you let the staff working there know, they will let you contact me there by phone."

Valerie handed Maria her card with her number on it. She thanked the woman and walked out of the alley slowly, catching her breath.

She walked through the streets back towards the crime scene where Charlie and Will were waiting. She knew they'd have to be fast to find the witness. A homeless drifter could leave the area any time. If they were to locate and question this Bill about the killer, they'd have to split up to find him.

# CHAPTER SEVEN

Valerie scanned the street in frustration as the occasional car passed by. Will stood beside her, looking around. His academic persona seemed out of place in surroundings like this. Buildings vacant, left to rot. And him with an immaculately pressed suit and bow tie.

"Where to next?" he said, trying to catch his breath.

They had headed out from the murder scene due east together. Charlie, on the other hand, had headed west, exploring some of the less traveled parts of town a few streets over.

So far, Valerie and Will had been down two different alleyways and had stopped to question several homeless people who hung around on the streets in that area. But none of that had produced a lead. The witness Valerie needed to find, Bill, was as elusive as the killer.

"They all seem so frightened of us," Valerie said, sighing. "Even if they did know where Bill was, it feels like most of them wouldn't want to talk to us. It's frustrating."

"You have to look at it from their perspective," Will said, still breathing heavily. "For many of these people, society has let them down. It has let them slip through the cracks, below which there should be a series of safety nets to protect the most vulnerable. But that's all gone. These people have been abandoned by society, Valerie. What do we represent to them?"

"Society itself," Valerie mused. "I suppose for them, law enforcement is just another system that hasn't helped. Another system that just throws them in jail when they step out of line, letting them die quietly out here in the forgotten parts of the city where no one looks. At least, that's how *they* must see it."

"Exactly," Will agreed. "And you know, in some ways it's true."

"You really believe that, do you?" Valerie asked, surprised. "When you spend most of your time studying at institutions, do you really think those institutions are failing people?"

"Sometimes two truths can appear at once, Valerie," Will said. "It's possible for a system to work for some, but not for others. It's possible for some to benefit, while others are held back or let down. Just look around you at the deprivation here. Boston is a beautiful, amazing city. But like every city, here we've been able to find the castaways."

"I've never really attached that to us in the FBI," Valerie said. " Not as a failing institution in terms of helping the poor. We just keep people safe. I've always thought that homelessness is more a failure of..." Valerie stopped going any further as she realized she was heading into territory where she might offend Will.

Will laughed. "You mean you think it's a failure of the mental health profession?"

"Studies show most people who are homeless have some sort of mental health issue," Valerie said, reluctantly. "I know it's difficult to tell whether that's because they develop those issues on the streets or it's the reason they end up there. But it does feel sometimes like they aren't getting the help they need."

"Perhaps we all fail them in our own little ways, without even realizing," Will said.

Valerie didn't answer that. She feared it was true. Whether failings were personal, societal, little, or large, no one was perfect. No system was perfect. And it pained her that so many could slip through the cracks. The world could be cruel sometimes. But she still believed in humanity's ability to help each other.

"But if I'm going to fail trying to help people," Will concluded. "I couldn't do it in better company." He smiled. It was a smile that somehow reassured Valerie. Will had all the affection, care, and wisdom Valerie wished she'd had in her life when she was younger. Listening to his words, he always found a way to put a positive spin on things. That really lifted people up.

Turning her thoughts back to canvassing the area for the witness, she wished she could find a way forward for them. A lead of some kind.

As if answering her thoughts, Will looked around and put his finger to his lips, tapping them as he often did when deep in thought.

"What are you thinking?" Valerie asked.

"We're always busy profiling killers," Will said. "Perhaps we should start profiling witnesses when we can't find them. What do you think?"

"That's an interesting idea," Valerie said. "What do you think about our witness, then?"

"Well," Will said. "We don't have too much to go on. We know that Bill is a homeless man. It seems that he's known on the streets well enough if what people are saying around here is anything to go by. That must mean that he's been homeless for a while. The woman that you spoke to, Marta, she seemed to like and trust him, implicitly. She said he was kind, didn't she?"

Valerie nodded in acknowledgment

"This would suggest that he might have few enemies out here, and a lot of friends. People may not want to talk with us. They might not want to betray Bill's trust. And as we mentioned before, we represent 'the man,' which puts us at a disadvantage to begin with: A lot of the homeless people don't trust the authorities."

"Where does that leave us and trying to track Bill down?" Valerie asked, feeling frustrated again.

"Use the techniques, Valerie," he said softly. "We can find him if we think like him. What sort of emotions are running through Bill's head right now? What would those emotions lead to in terms of his behavior?"

Valerie closed her eyes for a moment and blocked out her surroundings, mentally. She tried to put herself in Bill's shoes in the way she had put herself in the shoes of killers, murders, and fugitives several times before.

"He'd be scared," Valerie said. "He wouldn't trust anyone, especially us. Hiding would be his impulse…" Valerie could feel it working. Behind her eyes somewhere, the expert profiler was making herself known.

"Go on, don't lose track of it. Follow the thread," Will encouraged.

"If he's hiding, he wouldn't be down any of these alleyways. They are too out in the open," Valerie said. "And he'd associate them with the murder he witnessed. He would have to go… Somewhere he could truly feel secure. Like being under a warm blanket. He wouldn't be in the drop-in centers around here because they would know we would check them if he's thinking straight. But wherever he is hiding, it would have to cover him… It would have to be somewhere with a roof."

"I agree," said Will. "The need to hide when under threat is a distinctly primal one. Our brains seem hard-wired to seek out shelter in a specific way. It's certainly a survival mechanism. It probably dates back to early mammals, hiding in holes when predators were nearby."

Valerie looked at the streets around them. And then she saw it: a large bridge carrying a highway overhead in the distance. Something about it called to Valerie. She thought about Bill, about his desire to run, to hide. When she put herself in his mindset, it made perfect sense. A place shielded from the world, but not enclosed. Somewhere he could hide, but also somewhere he could easily escape from if the police came calling.

"The bridge..." Valerie said, crossing the street.

Will followed her as if implicitly trusting her powers of detection.

They moved with purpose, not running, but walking at pace. As the long street ahead of them curved around a corner, they found themselves standing across from the bridge. It cast a long, deep shadow, and on the outskirts of the underpass, Valerie could already see the cardboard boxes as evidence. Homeless people were using it for shelter.

"Keep your wits about you, Will," Valerie said. "I have nothing but sympathy for the people underneath the overpass, but walking around people who have been thrown away by society, sometimes that can be a dangerous journey."

Will nodded and then said: "I know..."

Will's voice trailed off, and in it, Valerie felt there was a story to tell. It was as though he had some experience of places like this. But this wasn't the time to delve into personal histories, at least not those unrelated to the case.

Though Will's forlorn expression as he looked at the people underneath the highway did make Valerie wonder about her friend and what he had seen in the past.

"Come on, Will," she said, gently, patting her friend on the shoulder.

He sighed and then looked up as if readying himself.

They walked across the street to the underpass, and as they did so, they felt the chill of its great shadow.

Valerie looked into the darkness as her eyes adjusted to it. She saw the remnants of a civilized world. Rows of people hiding as the roar of the highway above groaned like a ferocious beast.

People eyed Valerie and Will suspiciously as they passed. Most of them had dirtied faces, and there was a smell under there like people had been using part of the underpass as a toilet.

Valerie stopped for a moment. The air was cool yet rife. She tried to avoid the smells.

"Does anyone know a man named Bill?" Valerie said. Her voice bounced off the underside of the concrete and swirled around like a pinball.

She could hear people shuffling around in the shadows, could see a few moving behind pillars, others rolling over in blackened blankets pretending to be asleep.

No one wanted to answer her. She understood why. Bill, by the woman's account from the other alleyway, was well thought of. No one wanted to give him up.

Turning, she caught the stare of a young man. He barely looked old enough to be out of high school.

His hair was a mess of brown, but his eyes were bright. Valerie thought how handsome the man would have been, had he not been living in such squalor.

Valerie felt bad about using her profiling skills to identify weakness in someone so young, but she could tell by his body language. He both knew something and was frightened that Valerie would find out what it was.

She smiled at the man. He darted his glance away from her.

But it was too late for him, the connection had already been made.

Valerie moved towards him. She sensed a slight tremble in him, most probably from alcohol withdrawal.

"Hi," she said.

"H… Hi…" he answered, his voice trembling, too.

"My name is Valerie, what's yours?"

"Ricky," he said, not looking at her. Instead, he stared down at his feet. It reminded Valerie of a school child knowing they had done wrong but hoping to be left alone by the teacher.

"How long have you been here, Ricky?" Valerie asked. "I get the feeling it's not long."

"I dunno," he said. "A few weeks, maybe. I've lost track." He pointed to a blanket at his feet. Valerie could see a few empty bottles of cheap vodka hiding underneath.

"Hi, Ricky, I'm Doctor Will Cooper."

Ricky let out a nervous laugh. "You come to fix me, Doc? You come to fix all of us?" He pointed around at the huddled people watching from the shadows.

"I'd like to help," Will said, his tone a strange mix of care and sternness. "There was a murder…"

"I know," Ricky said. "We all know. Now what's anybody going to do about it?"

"It doesn't sound like you think that's unusual," Will observed.

Ricky scoffed in disbelief. "Every week one of us disappears or ends up dead somewhere, and what do the cops do? Nothin'. But I hear this girl wasn't one of us. Now I bet some pristine woman gets killed walkin' around in the wrong neighborhood, and *everyone* will suddenly care that there's a serial killer on the streets of Boston."

Valerie's ears perked up. "You think there's a serial killer?"

"Well, duh," Ricky said. "How do you explain all the people disappearin' on the streets?"

"Homeless people sometimes drift from one place to another," Will answered. "They are difficult to track. They could just have headed somewhere else."

Ricky grew visibly annoyed. "You think I'm makin' any of this up?"

"No," Valerie said, softly. "We're here to catch the person who murdered that girl. But we do think he might be a serial killer."

Ricky eyed Will suspiciously, but he seemed to be responding to Valerie's line of questioning. He stepped in closer, his face just an inch from Valerie's. His eyes darted left to right as if about to say something forbidden. And then he spoke into her ear as if he didn't want anyone to know what he was saying.

"I see him in my dreams," he said. "He creeps around and comes out at night. He watches us all. Then he picks who he's going to take and then they disappear while they sleep."

Ricky pulled back nodding and staring at Valerie intently. His gaze then momentarily flickered to somewhere behind Valerie in the darkness. Just over her right shoulder and behind a pillar. But the expression on his face wasn't one of fear. It was one of friendship and care.

The man wasn't hallucinating something frightening; he was seeing something close to him.

Valerie knew two things from the way Ricky was behaving. The first was that he was suffering from paranoid delusions. Night terrors were common among those abusing alcohol. At night their bodies would go into withdrawal and the hallucinations would come.

The second thing Valerie knew now, beyond a shadow of a doubt, was that Bill was somewhere in the underpass. She gauged this from where Ricky had looked behind her.

"We'll do everything we can to catch the killer," Valerie said, putting her hand slowly into her pocket.

"Thank you," Ricky said. "We're scared."

She watched again, closely. The angle of Ricky's stare as it moved behind her again…

Valerie spun around and pulled her flashlight out of her pocket in one smooth motion. With the click of a button it came on, and Valerie shone its beam to the side of a giant stone pillar.

A face peeked out from behind it.

"Bill?" Valerie said.

"Leave me alone! I didn't do anything!" the man yelled, and darted behind the stone pillar quickly.

Will and Valerie sprung forward, arching around the stone, but by the time they reached it, they found they were faced by several more stone pillars, looming in the distance underneath the highway.

Footsteps pounded somewhere under the bridge, the sound ricocheting about. The noise echoed so much off of everything around her, Valerie couldn't tell which way Bill had run.

Looking around at the faces of the homeless people sheltering under the bridge, she knew they wouldn't help her out of loyalty to their friend.

"Which way?" Will said, his voice sounding desperate.

"I don't know."

But Valerie couldn't stand still. She closed her eyes for a moment and listened to the echoing footsteps getting farther away. It was a guess at best, but she rushed forward, flashlight in hand, and chased after Bill, hoping he would know something about the murder.

# CHAPTER EIGHT

Charlie was blocking out the misery of it all. The sadness of Boston's homeless littering that dilapidated part of town.

He knew Valerie and Will were only a couple of streets away at their last check in, but he was astounded by how different the street was where he now found himself.

It was a relic of the past. Ornate buildings once housing prospering businesses, were now shuttered and dying. Patches of damp from rain had fed mold on the sandstone and granite. High up above, carefully crafted cherubs looked down.

Once they would have been clean and pure, but now their faces were covered in grime. They opulence of the past in that street had faded, replaced only by decay.

Charlie moved along it, hoping to find some clue to the witness's whereabouts.

Most of the windows were boarded up around him. There were several condemned signs plastered around in red. But as far as he could see, the wrecking crews were nowhere to be seen.

Passing a doorway in the gray light, Charlie found an old man sitting in its shadows. He was wrapped in a blanket, even though it had been hot earlier in the day. The man's face was as worn as leather, a product of living outside for years on end.

Charlie wondered when the man had last felt the simple comfort of a bed.

"Excuse me, sir," he said.

The man looked up.

Charlie could see the look on his face more clearly. The gaunt, distant expression. He'd seen that look many times before. It was the look of someone on heroin.

His mind instantly jumped back to a guy in the neighborhood where he grew up called Tex, mainly down to the man's penchant for wearing cowboy boots.

That stood out in a neighborhood like that back in the day. But people liked Tex. He hung around with Charlie's brother Marvin.

Charlie would never forget the night Tex overdosed and Marvin came running to him for help.

The fear in his brother's eyes still haunted him. What haunted him more, however, was the fact that the same terror, the same fear of bad things happening, soon melted away from Marvin after that. He lost his fear for consequences.

"Hey, sonny," the old man in the doorway said. "You okay?"

Charlie realized that, for a moment, he'd been caught in thought. That was dangerous. Charlie didn't like being distracted from his environment. But his brother's sudden reappearance was having that effect.

"Sorry to bother you, sir," Charlie said, snapping out of it. "But I'm looking for a man named Bill. He sleeps around this part of town. We're concerned for his welfare."

"I know a couple of Bills," the old man said. "Bill Creed, Bill Lane, Bill Jolson…"

"Have you noticed anything strange about any Bill around here? After last night?"

"You know who my favorite Bill is?" the old man asked.

Charlie shook his head.

"Dollar Bill." The man grinned, revealing no teeth.

Charlie laughed. He had to give it to the old fella. He was hustling. Charlie took out his wallet and put a twenty into the old man's hand.

"Yeah, I heard the rumors," the old man said. "Bill Creed seen something nasty in one of the alleyways off of Jermaine Street. He cut through here and headed for Maxwell Bridge."

"Maxwell Bridge?" Charlie asked.

The old man pointed a few streets away to the highway exit, lurching upward. "It's under that monstrosity. I don't sleep around there, though. It's too damp for my old bones."

"Thanks," Charlie said. He looked around and stepped to move further down the street.

"Sonny," the old man interjected. "Don't be walking down there, that's a dangerous place. Head around the corner on Maple. It's a little longer, but safer."

"I don't have time to wait. But thanks." Charlie felt touched that the old man would try to stop him coming to harm. So he put his hand in his pocket and pulled out another twenty, giving it to him before heading down the street.

Down the exact route towards the bridge in the distance, where the old man said he shouldn't step foot.

*

Charlie had been moving at pace towards the bridge for at least ten minutes. And with each step, he came to understand the old man's warning. The road narrowed, and the dilapidated buildings felt like they were closing in on Charlie.

He saw two separate groups of men hanging on street corners, and they eyed him suspiciously as he passed. That was okay. The feeling was mutual. Charlie could smell a drug gang a mile off.

He didn't want to be on that street for much longer and hoped he could quickly reach its end soon, moving into a more populated area around Maxwell Bridge.

The shuttered windows and shadowy doorways of the street passed by at speed as Charlie picked up the pace.

His mind wandered again to his brother for a moment. That area was exactly the type of place he'd always worried Marvin would end up. But now he was saying he was reformed. That he was legitimate.

In his heart, Charlie hoped that was the case. But he couldn't bring himself to believe it. Not yet. He'd been pulled into one too many scrapes by his brother over the years. Charlie wondered if a leopard really could change its spots. The world had taught him it was unlikely.

Rushing out from a nearby doorway like a blur, a stocky man suddenly shoulder barged Charlie from the side.

Charlie hadn't been paying attention. And now he would have to settle that bill.

He felt a blinding pain as the man's shoulder thrust sharply into him. Charlie had been moving at speed, and so he completely lost balance and fell to the street, tumbling over.

His training kicked in as he fell. He reached up and cupped the back of his head with his hands, and pulled his elbows up alongside his temples. Charlie's body cracked off the broken sidewalk. It was painful. But at least he was conscious.

The man who had attacked him now rushed over to Charlie and thrust out his foot.

Charlie rolled to the side, evading the heel that may have landed squarely on his right eye.

"Give me yer wallet!" the figure said.

"Okay… Okay… Okay…" Charlie said, reaching into his pocket and holding up his wallet.

The man snatched it from him.

"Open it," Charlie said.

"What?" the man replied, adrenaline clearly coursing through his body. He opened the wallet and his eyes flickered with fear.

Charlie knew what he was staring at. It was an FBI badge. He quickly pulled out his gun from its holster and pointed it upwards at his attacker.

"Son," Charlie said. "You just picked the wrong person to rob."

The man dropped the wallet and raised his hands over his head.

Charlie raised up onto his feet, never taking his aim off the man for a moment. He wasn't the killer, just a pathetic robber, but Charlie looked forward to putting him in cuffs so he couldn't rob anyone else.

"Turn around," Charlie said. "Put your hands behind your back."

A simple click, and Charlie had put the cuffs on the man. "I might be having a bad day, pal. But yours just got far worse. You just assaulted and tried to rob a Federal agent while he was on duty. I think you can say 'bye-bye' to sunlight for a while."

"I didn't mean it, man!" the man howled. But Charlie didn't fall for that. He had nothing but sympathy for someone who was homeless and had fallen on hard times, but this guy was a criminal. He'd seen that look in the man's eyes. He enjoyed robbing people. Well, not anymore.

"If I wasn't chasing down a lead, I'd take you in myself," Charlie said, still wincing from the pain in his ribs. "But I have bigger fish to catch."

"You… You gonna let me go then?" the attacker said, hopefully.

"Come here." Charlie led the man by the arm over to the side of one of the dilapidated buildings. He started pulling on an old fence. A couple of the rails came off, but when he found one that wouldn't budge, he cuffed the man to it.

Charlie took out his phone and dialed the local police department. He caught his breath as it rang.

"District B-2 Police Department, how can I help?" the voice said on the other end of the call.

"This is Agent Charlie Carlson with the FBI," Charlie began. "I have apprehended someone who tried to rob me on Poe Avenue. I've cuffed him to a railing outside number 62. But I'm on a case, so I'll have to process him with you later. Can you send someone over to pick him up?"

Charlie gave the rest of his details and, eventually, the police department agreed to send someone around, although it was highly irregular.

After hanging up, Charlie walked back over to the cuffed attacker, who, after trying to pull at the railing while Charlie was on the phone, gave up, knowing it wouldn't give.

"Hang tight, pal," Charlie said. "The Boston PD will come and take you to a nice, all-inclusive room with three meals a day and everything."

"You son of a..."

The man cursed everything under the sun, but Charlie wasn't going to hang around any longer. He had to move to Maxwell Bridge.

Moving along the street in the same direction, the bridge loomed closer than it had, but Charlie couldn't move as fast as he had before. He'd need to ice his ribs when they got settled into their hotel room.

Just as he was feeling a little worse for wear, his phone rang. It was Valerie.

"Hello?" Charlie said as he moved along the street.

"Charlie!" Valerie sounded breathless. "I've flushed Bill Creed out from under Maxwell Bridge. I think he might be heading in your direction. Are you near Whitmore Crescent?"

"Hold on..." Charlie fumbled with his phone, looking at a map of the area. "Yeah. Not far!"

"He's wearing a long brown coat and dirty white sneakers. I'd say he's in his early thirties."

"I'm on it!"

"Meet you there!" Valerie said.

Charlie hung up and found that the adrenaline was now enough to push him on. He moved quickly, scanning the street as he did so. Soon he saw the corner he was looking for, and found himself moving down an alleyway and hurdling a bunch of black trash bags that had been left out.

He darted between a collection of trash and other debris that had been dumped in the alley until he emerged on the other side.

Across the street, he saw a sign clinging for dear life to another street.

"Whitmore Crescent," he said to himself as he rushed across to where it began.

But as he did so, his keen hearing picked up on something. His footsteps were not the only ones.

A second set of footsteps now echoed between the buildings. They sounded panicked. They sounded frantic. The sounded, to Charlie, like those of someone running away from a great threat.

He was certain that the perceived threat was Agent Valerie Law relentlessly, courageously chasing down her man.

Charlie moved down the street and listened. The footsteps were getting closer. He ducked down behind a parked car for cover and peered over the hood.

He couldn't see anyone coming, yet.

Quickly and quietly, he kept himself as hidden from sight as possible, moving from car to doorway, and then between another two parked vehicles.

It sounded like the footsteps were upon him. But the echo in the street made the timing uncertain. Charlie had to use his other talents. He put his back against a parked van and then waited.

He kept switching his gaze from a window nearby to the windscreen of a car on the other side of the road, and then back again. If someone had seen him, they would have thought he was moving his head back and forth like a madman.

But Charlie wasn't disturbed. He was strategic. He was watching the reflection in the building window and in the car windscreen. Each gave him a view of what was going on behind him in the street.

Finally, in the car windscreen across the road, Charlie saw a moving blur racing down towards that side of the street. He knew he would have to be quick and time it perfectly. If he didn't, the man would see him and change his course, making him difficult to catch. And Charlie was already compromised after his altercation with the robber.

Hunkering down even lower, he moved back between the two parked cars and away from the van to get a better view. Peering over one of the cars, he could see the man coming, dressed in the long brown coat and white sneakers that looked like they had been left on the streets for an age.

It was him all right. It was Bill, and Charlie knew he couldn't let him slip by.

He rushed forward to the other side of the road and leaped over the hood of a parked red Ford, sliding on the surface and landing perfectly where the man was now running.

Charlie stood up, and reached out with his hands.

"Stop! FBI!"

He wrapped them around Bill Creed and picked him up in a vice-like bear grip. But Bill had instincts of his own. He smashed his elbows backwards. Normally, this would not have affected Charlie, but given the injury to his ribs he was already carrying, the sharp pain was too great.

Charlie fell back letting go of Bill. He crashed to the ground, lashing out with his hand and catching Bill's ankle.

Bill stumbled long enough for Charlie to rise back up to his feet. He rushed after the man, pulling him back by the coat. Bill swung around, catching Charlie on the chin, dazing him momentarily.

And in that moment, Bill spun around and started running again, but he was clearly disorientated. He started running in the opposite direction, back the way he had come.

Charlie shook his head and felt the light headedness of Bill's punch leave him. He pushed on after the man, following as best he could.

As Charlie ran after Bill Creed, Charlie became aware of someone shouting. It was Valerie. Bill was running straight towards her.

He seemed to realize this at the last moment and tried to squeeze between two closely parked cars, moving towards a patch of grass in a small park. But Valerie wouldn't let him. She was relentless. She cut him off at the entrance of the park and swept the man's leg.

Bill Creed fell crashing to the ground, and in moments, Charlie had caught up, pulling the man to his feet as Valerie cuffed him.

"Where are your cuffs?" Valerie asked, panting.

"A long story," said Charlie.

Will soon followed, looking like he was going to drop from exhaustion.

"You… You caught him then…" he said, gasping.

"Bill Creed is his full name," Charlie said. "I met someone back there who told me."

"Well, Bill Creed," Valerie said, still trying to calm her breath. "It looks like we need to have a little chat about the woman who was murdered last night."

Bill Creed looked forlorn, and Charlie started to hope that they hadn't just caught a witness, but the actual murderer instead.

# CHAPTER NINE

Valerie stared at the restroom, waiting for Bill Creed to come out. Above, a fluorescent light flickered slightly, and the air conditioning in the building seemed to be malfunctioning, as it was blisteringly hot.

Will and Charlie were in the restroom with Bill Creed, helping him get changed after his shower and cleaned up.

Balenthaul Police Department was located on the south side of Boston, and when they had arrived there with Bill Creed to question him, Will was quite insistent that the man be afforded every possible kindness.

Although it wasn't procedure, Valerie had backed Will up when talking with the duty sergeant, using the rationale that Bill Creed might give them the identity of the killer if he were treated with dignity.

But what had struck Valerie was how forceful Will was about it. Again, she felt as though he had a deep, personal connection to Bill's situation, and that was something she would need to ask him about at a later date.

In Valerie's mind, she was at least certain the man wasn't the killer. A casual look at him and conversation had assured her of that. It was her job to profile people. This man was a frightened witness, not someone compelled to kill. Besides, he didn't have nearly enough blood on him.

The door to the restroom opened and Bill Creed walked out, still in cuffs. But he'd had a shave and a shower. He was also wearing some new clothes Charlie had run out to get for him.

All in all, Bill Creed looked like a new man. Except in the eyes. He was frightened. He had seen something, and Valerie wanted to know just what.

*

Valerie sat across the interview table from Bill Creed. She had gotten him a cold drink to counter the failing AC at the police station. The interview room was bland, with pale blue walls that almost looked sickly.

Bill guzzled down the drink as though it had been an eternity since he'd had one.

It was a busy room. Charlie and Will were sitting on either side of Valerie, and behind them, Detective Monaghan was standing in the corner.

His hands were in his pockets, and he was fidgeting like he was counting down the seconds to his next cigarette. But Valerie was glad he was there. As long as he didn't get in the way, he could provide some keen local insight.

"Is it good?" Will said with a kind smile.

Bill took a look at the fizzing drink in his hand. He nodded. "Thanks, Doctor."

"Please, call me Will."

"Thank you, Will." Bill took another drink.

"Mr. Creed," Valerie began. "Why did you run from us?"

"I... I knew you were going to pin what happened on me."

"Well, it certainly looks bad when you run and then assault a Federal agent," Charlie said.

"I didn't know you were a Federal agent; you didn't tell me. You just ran out and grabbed me."

"Is this true?" Monaghan said from behind.

Charlie sighed. "Yeah. Yeah it is."

Valerie thought this was unusual for Charlie.

He normally was as methodical as they come. She didn't want to dwell on the mistake, however, as it would make him look bad. And Valerie thought Charlie was the most capable agent she'd ever met.

"Bill," Will said, softly. "I'm sure Agent Carlson will let that misunderstanding slide, if you're honest and helpful with us."

Charlie nodded.

"Mr. Creed," Valerie interjected, wanting to steer the interview to the murder. "What happened last night?"

"I.. I saw a young woman... She was beautiful. But I knew she was out of place. She wasn't one of us."

"One of us?" Monaghan asked gruffly.

"Homeless folk," Bill said. "You could spot her a mile off. I knew something wasn't right."

"Like what?" asked Valerie.

"She had a look on her face, like she was scared. I don't blame her. I remember my first night walking the streets. Scared the hell out of me."

"And how did you end up on the streets?" Will asked.

Valerie was a little perplexed. Will was asking questions about Bill Creed's history. That was a good way to get someone to open up, but Bill was already opening up. He was already answering their questions. Yet Will seemed preoccupied with learning more about the man.

"Yeah, I've been on the streets for some time," Bill said. "The first night was when I ran away from my foster home."

"Maybe you should have stayed there, then," Detective Monaghan said.

Will turned and gave the detective an accusatory glare. Valerie had never seen him like that before. If she hadn't known Will better, she would have thought he was about to stand up and slug Monaghan in the mouth.

There was an uncomfortable silence for a moment before Will returned to his more cordial self.

"Foster homes can be rough if you don't get the right foster family," Will offered.

"Damn straight," said Bill. He scratched his chin and looked at his hands. "Some families are good. Some are bad, I guess. Mine went bad. My foster dad, he was too handy with a belt." Bill turned his hands over and showed long scars on the palms of his hand.

"I'm so sorry," Will said, distantly.

Valerie felt the emotion running through Will. The interview was in danger of going off the rails.

"Mr. Creed," she said. "The woman you saw last night, what happened?"

Bill sighed and then rubbed his face nervously. He looked distraught. "I wouldn't want those streets to swallow up a young woman like that. I've seen it too many times. So I followed her. And… I just wanted to speak with her, tell her to get out before that place got her. Tell her to find somewhere safer for the night."

"And did you speak with her?" Charlie asked.

"No," Bill said pointedly. "I didn't get a chance. We got to a quiet part of an alley and… My God…"

"It's okay, Mr. Creed… Bill…" Valerie said. "Please go on."

"Someone stepped out of the shadows. They had a knife. Before I knew what had happened, I was covered in the woman's blood. She was dead."

"Did you get a good look at the killer?" Monaghan piped up from the corner.

"I know it sounds strange," Bill said. "But when I try to think about him, I can't really see his face. But I did look at it."

"It's quite common for the mind to blot out important details when under this much stress, Bill," Will offered.

"Did you see what he was wearing?" Charlie asked.

Valerie knew what Charlie was trying to do. Sometimes connected details could reignite a person's memory.

"He was dressed in a dark jacket... I think..."

"Probably another bum going off the rails," Monaghan said.

Will glared at him again.

"You know, Doctor, you keep glaring at me like that, you and me are liable not to see eye to eye," Monaghan said, the threat clear in his voice.

Charlie turned to Monaghan. "And if someone gets rough with Will, they get rough with me."

Monaghan and Charlie stared at each other. But Valerie could see that the detective wasn't about to challenge him. Charlie could be very imposing when he wanted to. It warmed her heart to know he had Will's back. The three of them had grown very close, and Will was now every bit their partner as much as Valerie and Charlie were to each other.

"Guys, let's not lose our professionalism," Valerie said trying to cool things down. "The killer is the enemy."

Valerie turned back to Bill. "Excuse us, Bill. We're all a little tense. We really want to catch this killer so he doesn't murder anyone else."

Bill looked shocked. "You... You think he's going to do it again?"

"I think so," answered Valerie. "Do you have any idea about his age?"

Bill closed his eyes as if thinking through those moments in the alley. "He was taller than me, maybe just under six foot. Lean. White. His hair looked dark, but it was difficult to tell. It was ruffled up a bit. He could have been from the streets, but he could have just been someone down there preying on people like me. It happens all the time, but the police turn a blind eye to it."

"We do not!" Monaghan said, sharply.

"Whenever someone goes missing from the streets," Bill continued. "There's never any fuss about it. We're not worth the same to the world as people who have homes and work, I guess."

"We do everything we can, Mr. Creed," Monaghan replied. He sighed. "I gotta get some fresh air." He walked out of the room.

"He's a barrel of laughs," Bill said.

"I think he's just frustrated we haven't caught this guy yet," Valerie explained. "Can you remember anything else about the killer?"

"No," Bill said, his voice mournful. "Just his eyes. His awful stare. I can tell you one thing though, he might have been standing in the shadows, but he didn't care if anyone saw."

Valerie sat back for a second to think. Bill's description was so generic. The killer could have been practically anyone.

"Hang tight, Bill," she said, standing up and walking towards the door.

"If you don't mind," Will said. "I'd like to stay and chat with Bill."

"I'd like that," Bill said.

"No problem, Will." Valerie then left the room with Charlie following suit.

They walked along the corridor and then stood by a vending machine. Valerie took out some coins and put them into the machine. The coins slid down straight to the bottom and out to the return slot.

"Damn," she said.

"The case or the fact you can't get a Twinkie?" Charlie asked.

Valerie turned to her partner. "I'm worried about this killer, Charlie."

"We've been here before," he said. "We deal with the worst kind."

"I feel like this one is different, Charlie. He's a walking contradiction. He likes the shadows, but he doesn't care about being seen. He kills quickly, but violently. He leaves a witness when he has an opportunity to kill him, too. Was he stalking the girl or waiting for her? Did he know her? Is he a predator or an opportunistic killer?"

"We can't answer any of those because we don't have enough data on the killer yet," Charlie said. "We need more information about how he kills to build a profile."

"Maybe," Valerie said, sighing. "Or maybe he's more unpredictable than the others."

"It's not like you to get this spooked."

Valerie felt that, too. She was normally calm and collected. But she was frayed at the edges. She saw her faint reflection in the glass of the vending machine. She looked gaunter to herself. She couldn't tell if it was in her mind or not.

"Maybe none of us are what we seem," she said. The words slipped out, unintended. She had spoken them quietly, but there was no doubt Charlie heard her.

She turned and looked at him. But he had an unusual look on his face. If Valerie didn't know any better, she would have concluded that Charlie thought she was talking about him.

"Ignore me, Charlie," she said. "I'm just not in a great place right now."

"I know, Val. How are things with your family?"

"Not the best," she said. "I found my dad finally."

"That's great!"

"But... It's complicated," she said. "I just really want to focus on the case for now. It keeps me sane."

Charlie laughed. "You and me both."

*But you don't know, Charlie. I'm not joking. Sanity is in short supply right now*, she thought.

"So, what now?" Charlie asked.

"I think you're right about needing more data," she said. "We need to check out the first victim. Maybe we'll have a better handle on the killer, then."

Deep down, Valerie still had that feeling. That sense that the killer wasn't going to be as predictable as others. She couldn't quite put her finger on why. She hoped that investigating the first murder would prove her wrong, but in her heart she believed that there would be more pain ahead for everyone involved.

For the victims, for their families, even for the investigators, something wicked was on its way.

And Valerie knew she would have to meet it head on.

# CHAPTER TEN

The killer felt the rain on the back of his neck. Its icy coldness fingered its way down his pale skin. But he didn't mind. He liked the cold. It was one of the reasons he was able to mingle with the homeless so easily.

His feet carried him onward through the wet evening, walking past countless strangers who all tried to shield themselves from the elements. He wondered if they knew as they passed him. Could they tell they had just brushed shoulders with someone who had committed murder?

He wasn't scared of getting caught. At least, not for the usual reasons. He'd always hated how much people feared being locked up. But he had experienced that before. Places like that didn't scare him. But what did, was not being able to touch the past again.

His feet carried him onward…

Yes, the past, that was where he was heading. A traveler of sorts. Not through time, but through memory. And the places he wished to visit would bring those memories to the forefront. They would let him relive those milestones. To close his eyes and think of them. To hear the sounds. To feel the importance of it all.

His feet carried him onward…

The knife in his pocket felt heavier than usual. It was as though it were picking up pieces of his victims, taking in a shattered remnant of their souls.

But he tried to shy away from that sort of thinking. That was what had gotten him into trouble before. That was what had led to the head doctors and their manipulative ways.

Yes, he had to keep his mind straight.

He crossed the road. Cars passed behind him swishing through puddles, moving off to unknown destinations. But the killer, he knew his destination fine and well. It was a special place. And if anyone was there to disturb his connection to it… He grinned to himself, feeling the knife in his pocket again.

*I'll cut them open like the rest.*

# CHAPTER ELEVEN

Valerie sat in the passenger seat of the car and watched the rain cascade down the window. Charlie sat next to her, moving carefully through the sheets of water, gazing occasionally at the GPS on the dashboard. They were on their way to visit the killer's first known crime scene, the first murder that started all of it.

Looking through the rain, Valerie was in a daze. Her mind was being pulled back again to thoughts of her dad.

*Why won't you just take the test?* she thought. Valerie was still at a loss to understand it. For a man who had abandoned her as though she were nothing, her father sure seemed intent on maintaining his claim to being her biological dad.

As Valerie's thoughts moved between her dad, to the case, and then back to her dad again, she suddenly realized she was staring into the wing mirror. It too was covered in beads of rain, but in the reflection, she could see partially see Will.

He was leaning with his head against the glass, looking as disconnected from the world as Valerie felt.

"Will, are you okay?"

"Huh?" he said, breaking out of his daze. "Oh… Right, yes, thank you. Quite all right."

Valerie waited for a moment. She was concerned for Will. Ever since he had laid eyes on Boston's homeless population, he hadn't been himself. It was as though it had sparked a deep wound within him, opening it up again.

And then there was his attitude towards Bill Creed.

Will had wanted to talk to the man more like a therapist than an investigator tracking down a serial killer. Then there was the way he had defended Bill. Sure, he had only glared at Detective Monaghan's gruff, perhaps even prejudiced, approach to the homeless, but that was pretty aggressive for the lovable academic.

"Will," Valerie said, turning to look at him in the back seat. "I hope you don't mind me asking, but back there at the interview with Bill Creed… You seemed connected to him somehow."

"I'd never met him before."

"I know," Valerie said. "But I just felt that his situation, something about it upset you, and I guess I wanted to make sure you were okay."

"I have to say," Charlie said, finally breaking his long silence. "That I noticed it, too, Will. If there's something about this case that's getting under your skin, you know you can talk to us about it. We might be able to help."

Will lifted his left hand up and tapped his cheek a few times with his index finger. He was always doing that sort of thing when nervous. Valerie knew that touching your face during times of anxiety, was a way to self soothe. It imitated the way that parents sometimes affectionately pat their children when they are upset.

"I'm quite fine, I assure you."

But Valerie didn't believe that. Sometimes people needed a little prod for their own good. This was one of those times.

"Did you know someone who was homeless?" she asked.

Will looked at Valerie. He had the expression of someone on the brink of saying something deeply personal.

And then Valerie's phone rang. She sighed in frustration and looked down at it.

"It's Tom," she said.

"You better get it," Will said.

"I can call him back, Will. I…"

"Speak with your fiancée, Valerie."

Valerie knew the moment of truth had passed. She could see Will closing up to her again.

She turned to face the rain covered windscreen and answered her phone.

"Hey, Tom," she said.

"Hi, Val, you okay?" he said on the other end of the line.

"Yeah… I'm fine. We're just en route to a crime scene. Everything okay with you?"

"Well," he said. "I've been having a think."

"Always dangerous," Valerie joked.

"Very funny… But I want you to hold off on telling anyone about our engagement. I think it's only right that I tell my parents first. I know it sounds old fashioned, but I want them to know before anyone else."

Valerie's heart sank. Charlie and Will already knew. She couldn't be certain, but Charlie could have phoned or messaged Angela with the good news as well.

"Oh…" Valerie said, not wanting to lie. Omission wasn't quite deception. "I thought you would have phoned them by now."

"That's the thing," Tom said. "I was going to, but I know they'll be disappointed."

"You really know how to make a girl feel special."

"Again, your humor slays me," Tom laughed. "No, what I mean is: They're kind of old fashioned about this sort of thing and I think they'd be hurt if I just told them over the phone."

"I can't get the time off right now, Tom…" Valerie felt uncertain about everything as it was, but even if she hadn't been on a case, being there in person to announce the engagement would have made it all a bit *too* real. She liked Tom's family, a lot, but she wanted to get used to being engaged before having a hundred questions about a far off, distant wedding in the future.

"You don't need to come with me, Val," Tom said. "I know you can't get away. Like I said before, I get it. I'll have to get used to being the life partner of an FBI agent. But I still need to go. So, I wanted to let you know I'll be flying out tonight to see them for a few days."

Valerie was relieved in a way that he wasn't asking her to go with him. With everything that was going around in her mind, she didn't want to have a meltdown like she did a while ago at their family table, and all because her family was too present in her mind.

But there was a profound conflict inside of her. A part of her knew she should be with Tom as he went, to celebrate, and perhaps to talk about what had been going on in her head. What fears she had for the future if her mental health declined. She felt like she was letting him down by not going with him.

She didn't say any of this, however. The conflict remained suppressed, pushed deep down inside.

"Okay, Tom. That's fine. Let me know when you've told them. Then I can start saying to people."

Charlie glanced at Valerie for a second from the driver's seat. He raised an eyebrow, clearly catching on to the fact that Tom had asked her to not let anyone know.

"I've got to go," she then said to Tom.

"Okay, Honey. I'll let you know when I've landed. Love you."

"Love you, too."

The call ended and Valerie put the phone back in her pocket. She looked out the windscreen as a gust of wind blew hundreds of raindrops across it. Charlie flicked the windshield wipers up a notch to deal with the increasingly bad weather.

"I might have texted Angela..." Charlie said.

Valerie sighed. "Okay. But I know she and Tom sometimes exchange recipes, so can you text her soon as we're at the scene to keep it under her hat?"

"Sure thing," Charlie said. He flicked on the indicator and exited the highway. "We'll be at the scene in a couple of minutes."

Valerie had to get her head back in the game. She took a deep breath and thought about the man in shadow. The killer in the alley. She hoped she could build a profile of the killer with new information about the first murder. If she couldn't, she had no idea how she was going to catch him.

# CHAPTER TWELVE

Valerie walked along Pearson Street, her two partners on either side of her. Boston was like any city. It had its beauty and its darkness. As Valerie looked around her to the run down area, populated by homeless people wandering now that the rain had stopped, she couldn't help but feel she was following the killer's shadow into the city's bleaker places.

Charlie pointed down a side street. "There, Beaumont Station. That's where the first victim was found."

The side street was even more dilapidated, and the few discount stores that were still doing business in that part of the city were closed for the evening. Valerie remembered an old George Romero film about the end of the world. The emptiness of that street reminded her of that. A place that had seen the end of things.

The three investigators stopped at the top of an escalator that led down underneath the street to Beaumont Station. A warm gust of air pushed out from it, like an animal breathing in its sleep.

"I've never liked subways," Valerie said.

"Me neither," Charlie replied.

"Oh, I don't know," said Will. "Subterranean places always fascinate me. There's another world down there, you know."

"You make it sound like the Morlocks live down there," Valerie joked.

"In some cities," Will said, his voice becoming tinged with sadness. "They call the homeless people who live in the tunnels and subways…"

"Mole people," Charlie said, finishing Will's sentence. "Labels are an easy way to dehumanize people."

"I couldn't agree more." Will winced slightly as if having an uncomfortable memory. "How far has society fallen that some feel the need to live where there is no sunlight?"

"We can only fix so many things ourselves, Will," Valerie said, trying to alleviate his discomfort. "Let's focus on stopping a killer. That's what we have power over right now."

Valerie walked down the stairs, the warm air continuing up to meet her. Will and Charlie followed.

The subway station was open, but she could see no human presence, at least at first. They walked through the brightly lit tunnels, their footsteps echoing and then deadening against the tight circular walls.

They came to a T-junction and Valerie looked up at the signs pointing in opposite directions. The green line and the red line.

"She was killed on the platform at the red line," Charlie said.

Following the sign to the left, Valerie thought it bitterly ironic that the red line led to the woman's death.

Opening up finally to the platform, Valerie observed that there was now no police tape. The platform was open as usual. In a small kiosk, a woman stood behind protective glass, selling tickets.

The only other person on the platform was a man in his sixties dressed in a t-shirt and jeans, and looking like he was going to nod off to sleep on one of the metal benches.

Taking her phone out of her pocket, Valerie searched for the file on victim number one. Identified as Alice Mayfield, she was 27 years old. A substitute teacher by profession, she was passionate about hockey and even played on a notable amateur team.

The notes on the file, written by Detective Monaghan, were helpful if a little underwhelming.

Looking at photographs of the scene, she pointed to down the platform.

"The body was found next to that corridor," she said. "The killer walked out from the opening and knifed her in the back. Then he wrapped his hand around her face from behind and slit her throat."

"The opposite direction," Charlie mused.

"What do you mean?" asked Will.

"He attacked victim 2 from the front, flicked the knife upward and then slit her throat," Charlie explained. "With victim 1, he attacked from behind, but still slit her throat."

"That tells us he's unpredictable," Valerie offered.

"And opportunistic," added Charlie. "I get the feeling he's not stalking these women. He's killing them on sight."

"Possibly," Valerie said, looking down at her phone again and perusing photos of Alice Mayfield's dead body when it was on the platform a couple of nights previous. "Let's take a closer look at where she was found."

"You're not press, are you?" a voice from the kiosk said as they walked by.

Valerie turned to the booth and saw a woman through the glass. "No, were FBI." She showed her ID.

"Good," the woman said. "I've had enough of those damn reporters down here. Buzzing around like flies, scaring people away."

"That many?" Charlie asked.

"You better believe it," said the woman. "All over the place. Even half of the regulars have left."

"Regulars?" Will asked. "You don't mean homeless people, by any chance?"

"That's a polite way to put it," the woman said. "I don't normally have them chased away. I figure they've been having a hard time as it is. They come down here to get out of the sun or get in from the cold when things freeze over. Bosses don't like it, but as long as I don't see them trying to walk on the lines down there, I turn a blind eye to it."

"Do you see them often doing that?" asked Valerie.

"Yeah, sure," the woman said. "There are so many tunnels and sewers in this city, you could get lost for days. Occasionally, I see someone jump off the platform and run into one of the tunnels. It's dangerous; we've had a couple get electrocuted by the line, another crushed by a train. But they still do it. I think there's a bit of a community down there. People living in forgotten parts of the system."

Valerie turned her gaze to the nearest open tunnel. She could hear in the distance a train grumbling.

"I wonder…" she said, turning back to her phone. She scrolled through some of Monaghan's notes. The CCTV footage of the murder couldn't tell where the killer had entered the subway station. Monaghan had written that he suspected the person entered alongside busy crowds so as not to be seen clearly.

"You don't think…" Will started.

"Maybe the killer came into the station from one of the tunnels," Valerie said.

Charlie grumbled. "That's a problem. He could disappear easily if he knows the layout. And he could come up practically anywhere in the city."

"And then disappear again…" Valerie was perturbed by this possibility. She switched over to the file for the second murder victim and then looked on a digital map of that part of the city. "I don't see a sub station near Maxwell Bridge…"

"Of course you don't," the woman behind the glass said. "But there used to be one. It shut down in the '80s. Those tunnels are still there, mind you."

"Thank you," Valerie said. "You've been a real help."

Valerie now walked with purpose over to the corridor where Alice Mayfield had been killed. Standing at the entrance of it, there was no evidence of what had occurred there. The body had been moved, the blood cleaned up, and there was no chalk line. People would have stepped over the tiled surface forgetting that the life of a young woman had been brutally taken there.

Looking onward, down the corridor that left the platform, it moved straight through to another one. Valerie moved along it, feeling the warm, stale air of the place caress her face and clothes.

She reached the other side of the corridor, emerging on the other red line platform. It allowed passengers to move in the opposite direction. It was almost a carbon copy but for one thing.

Valerie looked up and saw that the security camera was pointing at an unusual angle. She walked up to it and stood, carefully considering it.

Will and Charlie appeared behind her.

"What have you found?" Charlie asked.

Valerie turned and raised her hand and arm in a straight line. She closed one eye and looked along her arm with the other as if aiming.

"Hmmm," she said.

"Care to fill us in?" asked Will.

"This security camera," she said. "It's alignment is off. It covers the tunnel and most of the platform."

Valerie opened up her phone and looked through the file. There was a video file from some of the camera feeds on the platforms of the red line. It captured the platform in and around the time Alice Mayfield had been killed.

Clicking on the file, she watched the platform.

"Yes, look." She handed the phone to Charlie and Will.

"It cuts off part of the platform," Charlie said out loud.

Valerie moved along the platform at pace. She rushed along to the end of it just beside the tunnel. She then stood in the corner.

"Here!" she shouted enthusiastically, pointing to where she was standing. Her voice echoed along the empty platform. "This is the spot the camera can't see! I reckon it's been moved slightly to the left for that purpose at some point."

Valerie looked down at her feet. Beneath it was a metal plate with a handle on it. A warning emblazoned upon it said for maintenance purposes only.

"This should be locked..." she said to herself as she pulled at the handle. The plate gave way and, with some effort, it popped open. A breeze of cool air came up from inside.

Charlie and Will rushed over.

"My God," said Will. "What's down there?" Valerie took out her flashlight and shone it down inside. She could see a metal ladder affixed to the wall leading down a few meters into some sort of shaft.

"Looks like this heads down underneath the track," Valerie said. "It's awfully suspicious that the camera missed this."

"And that it's unlocked," Will observed. "The mechanism looks broken from the inside." He pointed to the underside of the hatch door. A small locking bar had been broken in two.

Valerie looked at it. She agreed. "It looks like it's been cut in two with something. A small hacksaw maybe. Something with a serrated edge."

"So," Charlie observed, "our killer comes here at some point, moves the camera to avoid that spot?"

"Just enough so that the security guards watching this feed wouldn't notice," Will offered.

"Then he was able to enter and leave the platforms quickly," Valerie said.

"This killer is a conundrum." Will looked worried. "He doesn't stalk his victims, as far as we know. He's opportunistic when he kills."

"And yet," added Valerie. "With the moving of the camera and the use of these tunnels, he's showing foresight and planning. It doesn't make sense. Killers are normally opportunistic or pre-planning. This killer is both."

Valerie closed the hatch and stood up.

"We're not going down there?" Charlie sounded surprised.

"You heard the lady in the kiosk," Valerie replied. "There are miles of tunnels under Boston. Countless maintenance hatches. Finding where he's been moving will be almost impossible."

"We should at least try," Will advised. "We might get lucky."

Valerie thought it over for a moment. "We have to be clever. There are only three experts on serial killers on this case. There are many

66

capable law enforcement officers who can explore these tunnels to see if anyone is using them."

"I can call Monaghan and get him to send some of his officers down here," Charlie offered.

"Great," said Valerie. "And get them to check the abandoned subway station over near Maxwell Bridge. Let's see if there's any evidence there of someone using it. The more I think about it, the more it makes sense. The killer was able to flee that alley and, as far as we know, he wasn't seen again after that. If there was an old maintenance tunnel he knew about, maybe he disappeared underneath, away from prying eyes."

"It's as good a theory as any," said Will. "But I am still worried about what our next move will be. The killer is contradictory. Opportunistic, yet with foresight. Uses the shadows and these tunnels, but then doesn't seem to be too careful in terms of being seen."

"You're worried about the profile?" Valerie asked.

"Yes," Will said, gravely. "We're going to have difficulty pinning this one down and predicting his behavior. I'm saddened to say that we might not be able to say more about him until he kills again."

Valerie wasn't used to Will being defeatist. It was as if the place was getting to him. The case had struck a personal chord with him, and this was dampening his spirits. She knew that she had to be the one to pull him out of it.

"We've got more than you think," she said. "We've got the world famous Doctor Will Cooper." She patted him on the back and smiled.

Will smiled back, but he seemed uncertain.

"Let's get back to the police station and work up a profile," Valerie said. Turning to the hatch for the last time, she thought about the killer lurking in the countless tunnels and maintenance shafts around the city.

*Where are you?* she pondered. But all that came to her was the sound of a subway train pulling into the platform, and the bleak darkness of the tunnel behind.

One thought remained on her mind:

*Just what kind of a killer are we dealing with here?* She had to find out.

# CHAPTER THIRTEEN

Valerie could hear the clock ticking in the background of the brightly lit police office. It seemed unusually loud as she poured over some old police records on the desk in front of her.

*Tick, tock.*

She tried to ignore it. But somehow the sound was getting louder in her head.

Balenthaul police station was now set up as their base of operations. Detective Monaghan had gotten the team some of the things they needed. But the office was cramped and almost claustrophobic with no windows.

To Valerie's side, Will was writing down some ideas and Charlie was on an old laptop scanning Boston's police records.

*Tick, tock.*

Valerie leaned back in her chair and tried to think. But it was no good. The ticking was incessant.

"Any luck, Charlie?" she asked, hoping that conversation would help.

Charlie didn't take his eyes off the laptop screen. "Still looking. This place is pretty antiquated."

And it was. Valerie was surprised that searching the police archives was so bothersome. But it had to be done.

"How far am I pushing the age range on the search criteria?" Charlie asked.

"No more than early forties," Valerie replied.

"I agree," Will said, sitting back in his chair and resting his pen on the desk. "I think he'll be anywhere from his later twenties to later thirties, but if we expand the search slightly, we might pick up an anomaly."

"The killer isn't textbook," said Valerie, her voice tired. "We should assume he won't fit any specific pattern. Most serial killers have reached an escalation point well before their forties, but who knows with this one."

"How are you faring?" Will asked.

"I was just reading some case files from the last decade I found in the archives here," Valerie replied. "Unsolved attacks. I was hoping to find someone with a penchant for quick knife kills. But nothing matches our guy, yet."

"Hmmm," Will replied, tapping his temple, deep in thought. "I still keep coming back to Bill Creed."

"You're not suggesting he did it?" Valerie asked, surprised.

"Oh no," he said. "But he told us the killer looked as though he *could* have been homeless, but not overtly in bad condition. My question is, are we looking for someone who knows the homeless scene in Boston and is able to move around it in predatory fashion?"

"He could be homeless," Valerie mused. "But…"

*Tick, tock. Tick, tock.*

Valerie lost her train of thought. She grew momentarily exasperated as she searched her mind for what she had been saying, hoping to get back on track before Will noticed. But the clock continued, incessantly. It moved precisely, the hands ticking around its face.

Valerie stared at it, and for a moment, she thought she saw something reflected in the glass of the clock: a dark shadow.

Looking around the room, she couldn't see what had caused it, but when she returned her gaze to the clock, the shadow was gone.

"What is it, Valerie?" Will's voice was etched with concern.

"Nothing," she said. "I just felt a chill." *Tick, tock. Tick, tock.*

*It's the illness*, she thought. *It's making me see things that aren't there. How bad will this get before they notice I'm losing it?*

"You were saying about the killer potentially being homeless?" Will prodded.

Finally, her mind snapped back to the word, back away from the ticking.

"He *could* be homeless," she repeated. "But I would have thought someone else would have seen him and named him by now if he was. When we spoke to Bill's friends before we caught up with him, they didn't seem to know the killer. They knew Bill because he was a regular around there. But they don't know the identity of the man killing right where they sleep. And then there's the mythologizing of this shadow moving around the streets killing people…"

"Do you really think he's been killing the homeless for a while and it hasn't registered?" Will asked.

"I don't know," said Valerie, looking back at the files in front of her. "I'd like to think not, but you've seen how those people are living.

The world has forgotten them. We get on with our lives and sleep in our beds. We live in the lap of luxury. How often do we think about the people living on the streets? Would we really notice if some disappeared or were killed?"

"It's a frightening thought," answered Will. "But I like to have more faith in the police here. Society might forget about those most in need, but the medics, the police officers, the social workers, I'm sure they would take notice if people started turning up dead."

"Okay," said Charlie. "I've actually found some matches on the police database."

Next to him, an old printer was busy spitting out a few pages. Charlie handed them to Valerie when they were done.

Valerie looked over them. They contained the records of several men, all white, all in the age group they would normally expect for such a killer.

"Maybe we'll get lucky," she said, trying to sound upbeat.

*Tick, tock. Tick, tock.*

She stared at the mugshots on the pages and tried to block out the clock as best she could. Time was indeed running out. Soon the killer would murder another innocent victim, and only Valerie and her team could stop him.

Standing up, Valerie turned to Charlie. "Is Bill Creed still in his cell?"

"Yeah," Charlie said. "He's staying voluntarily. Probably happy to have the bed. Monaghan kicked up fuss about it, said the station isn't a hotel. But I managed to talk him around to keeping Bill on sight in case anything jogged in his memory, and to save us from searching the streets for him."

"Good work, Charlie," Valerie said, still looking at the pages in her hands. "Come on, you too, Will."

Valerie opened the door of the cramped office and felt the still stale air of the station venture inward from the corridor. She walked at pace, and after a few twists and turns along bland corridors, she reached the back of the building where the cells were.

A police officer stood guard.

Valerie showed her badge. "I'm here to see Bill Creed. We're working with Detective Monaghan."

The officer nodded, turned, and then led the three FBI investigators to the door of cell number 3.

70

He knocked on the metal door and looked at the small square glass window which hung on it at head height. "Hey, Creed. The FBI want a word."

"Of course," came Bill's reply from the other side.

The officer opened the door and Valerie, Will, and Charlie all slipped inside to a small rectangular room with a toilet and a bed, and nothing else.

"Are they treating you okay, Bill?" Will asked.

"Sure thing, Doctor Cooper," he said. "It's better than sleeping on a sidewalk, I'll tell you that."

"Mr. Creed," said Valerie. "We have some mug shots here of people in the Boston area who have been investigated for previous crimes. Most of them involved threatening women with a knife. We wondered if you'd be okay to look at them to see if the killer might be among them?"

"Okay," Bill said, sounding uncertain.

Valerie handed the sheets of paper to him.

He looked them over, moving between them and studying the faces. "I really wish I could remember exactly what he looked like. But it's a blank, you know. I'm not sure if I saw him, I'd..." He trailed off.

Valerie felt a rush of excitement inside. She was watching Bill. And he was stuck on one photograph. Bill's face drained of color and his hands started trembling slightly.

"Do you see the killer, Bill?" Charlie asked.

"I can't be sure, but... It's this guy's eyes. They're so similar."

Valerie took the sheet from Bill and looked at the mugshot and attached information.

"Michael Shaw," she said out loud. "Previous for assault with a deadly weapon. He used a knife to rob a woman at night a few years ago. He got put away for it for a few years, but he was released just a few months ago." She looked up at Will.

"That would make sense," he said. "If this Michael Shaw is the killer, he probably tried to avoid his desires for a few months and then they finally took over. I've seen a case study on re-offending by the serial mindset."

"I've read that," Charlie said. "Written by a professor from California if I remember correctly."

Valerie smiled at Charlie. She couldn't hide her surprise at him nailing the academic side of the investigation. Will grinned.

"Don't patronize me," Charlie said. "I might not have a Ph.D. in profiling, but I do read up, you know."

"That's right though, Charlie," Valerie said. "I've read that paper, too. The average time for a released criminal who is escalating towards serial killer behaviors is about four months after release. That's spot on for this Michael Shaw."

"I hope you get him," Bill offered.

"So do I," said Valerie. "Thanks Mr. Creed... Bill..."

Valerie rushed out of the door and down the corridor as Will and Charlie followed quickly behind. It was 10PM, but sleep would wait. The killer, would not.

# CHAPTER FOURTEEN

Valerie thought the air was colder than it should have been. Night had well and truly fallen, and the shadows of the abandoned trailer park crept along the ground away from several tall street lights.

"I don't like the look of this place," Will said as they walked slowly down a dirt track.

"This is the last known location of Michael Shaw," Charlie reminded Will. "According to his parole record at least."

Valerie looked around at the large, open expanse of ground. Several rusted old trailers still stood, spread out from each other like islands of corrosion. Most of them appeared to be empty. Doors were broken off, windows smashed, dreams shattered.

"What happened here?" Will said out loud.

"Look over there." Valerie pointed to a large yellow sign that had rusted and fallen to the ground.

*Park closure for development.*

"That sign has been there for a while," Charlie observed.

"Same old story," Valerie added. "I remember something similar happening just outside D.C. The landlord of a piece of waste ground sold it to the local government. They said they were going to develop it into a mall and so moved everyone on. Eight years later, it's still empty as far as I know."

"But why?" asked Will, seemingly bemused.

"Because someone didn't like the trailer park and the people in it."

Charlie was looking around to several overgrown bushes that lined the path. "I don't like the feel of this place. Too many spots to hide."

Valerie knew that Charlie reverted back to his army training whenever there was uncertain terrain. But she didn't comment on his observation, even though she agreed with it. Valerie was increasingly aware that to utter a fear out loud was to feed it, at least when in the moment.

Dissecting one's fears was best done in a safe environment.

Valerie looked down at the land eviction sign as they passed it.

"Someone obviously came back here when it became clear the development wasn't happening," she theorized. "It's probably a quiet place for anyone homeless. Off the street, away from the danger."

"Away from the danger?" Charlie replied. "This place feels worse to me than the street. It's like something out of a Friday the 13th movie."

"Hopefully we don't run into any hockey mask wearing maniacs," Valerie quipped, patting Charlie on the shoulder. "I do take your point, though. I don't think we should fan out. Let's stick together and ask around; there are a few people obviously living here by the looks of things. We just need to find them."

Valerie moved forward down the path towards one of the trailers. The ground felt uncertain, with the soil and weeds growing out of a once graveled walkway.

She took out her flashlight and shone it inside through a broken window. The floor of the trailer was covered in mold and green weeds that had begun to reclaim it for nature's own obscured purpose.

Valerie was always amazed at how quickly humanity's world was subsumed by nature when left unattended.

"This one's empty," she said loudly. "Let's move on to the next one."

Charlie spun around. But Valerie had heard it, too. The sound of footsteps on the ground. And they did not belong to any of the three investigators.

"Kill the lights," Valerie said, and they each switched off their flashlights.

"Over there," Charlie said in a hushed tone.

Walking over to one of the rusted trailers some distance away was a man in a long coat. His hair was disheveled and he looked to be carrying a ruck sack on his back. The man moved towards the trailer, opened the door, and then went inside.

The door clattered as it closed.

"Did he see us?" Will asked.

"I don't think so," replied Charlie. "He seemed to be a little nervous the way he was looking around, but he was more worried about the entrance to the park in the opposite direction."

"We need to talk to him. Come on," Valerie said. "But stay sharp. I'm getting a bad feeling about this place the longer we stay."

They moved off the path and onto a wilder part of the ground that stretched between them and the trailer. Valerie noticed the difference in the ground. It was markedly more uneven, and at one time she reckoned it would have been a piece of landscaped garden or flower bed. Now it too had been reclaimed by the creeping undergrowth like everything else.

*More shadows here.*

That thought came and outstayed its welcome. Valerie was beginning to feel that when her mind grew tired, a paranoia about seeing things would emerge. And it was always worse in the darkness. In the darkness, your mind could easily build shapes out of anything.

As they approached the trailer, Valerie stepped forward, but Charlie held up his hand for a moment. "Let's be careful going in there. If we're feeling nervous out in a place like this, anyone in there might feel the same way. It's not a good idea to stoke that fire."

"Agreed," Valerie said quietly. "We don't want whoever is in there to freak out and come charging at us. Agent Philips comes to mind."

"Who is Agent Philips?" Will asked.

"A colleague of ours," Valerie replied. "Ended up taking a blast from a sawed off shotgun because he was overly brash."

"That's exactly what one wants to hear in a situation like this," Will said, the anxiety clear on his face.

"We just need to announce ourselves first," Valerie said, stepping a little closer to the trailer but off to the side of the door.

She looked at Charlie to make sure he was ready. Charlie nodded, then she turned back to the trailer. "Hello? My name is Valerie. I'm with the FBI. Can we ask you a few questions?"

There was a clatter inside, like someone had kicked over a bag full of old tin cans.

"Eh... I'd rather not," a voice said from inside.

"And why is that?" Valerie asked.

"How do I know you're really FBI," the voice said. "For all I know you're that maniac going around offing people from the streets."

"I'm going to approach the door and slide my ID underneath," Valerie said. She took out her ID and pushed it through a gap at the base of the door. She hoped she'd get it back. She'd lost her ID and badge once during a fight with a fugitive in a sewer once, and her boss Jackson wasn't happy about that.

The man cursed under his breath from behind the door.

"Okay... Okay," he finally said. "What do you want?"

"First, my ID back," Valerie said.

The ID slid out back to her from under the door.

"Second," she continued. "We'd like to have a friendly chat about someone we think might be living on this site."

"I... I don't know many people around here," the voice replied, nervously.

"Let's start with first names," Valerie said, trying to calm the conversation. "My name is Valerie. And you are?"

"Eh... Pete."

Valerie could hear in the hesitation that he'd given a fake name. But she wasn't going to bite on that.

"Okay, Pete," she said. "It's nice to meet you. Is there any chance you could open the door so we can chat?"

"I... I don't think I'd like that. I just want to be left alone."

Something clattered from the other end of the abandoned trailer park. Valerie instinctively turned towards it. But all she could see were the rusting trailers and empty patches of ground occasionally lit by the remaining few street lights that still worked.

She wondered if she had been hearing things, but Charlie seemed to grow agitated by the noise.

"Listen, Pete," he said. "We can do this the friendly way or the unfriendly way."

"What's the difference with the FBI?" Pete said from the other side of the door.

"Let me educate you," Charlie said. "The friendly way is you open this door, we ask you a few questions about someone who is supposed to be staying in this park, and then we'll be on our way, never to darken your doorstep ever again."

"And... The unfriendly way?" the man asked, hesitating.

"I can lift this door off its hinges with my bare hands and then I can drag you in for obstructing Federal agents in their business."

Valerie was surprised at Charlie. He was often jovial, often diplomatic, but there was something working at him. She'd sensed it since the beginning of the case. He'd briefly mentioned issues with his brother, and she suspected it was that, but she hoped he would open up about it more when they had some down time.

She felt guilty for almost feeling relieved that she wasn't the only one having family issues. She wouldn't have wished that on Charlie, but there was camaraderie in shared problems like that.

"So what's it going to be, buddy?" Charlie asked.

"I'd do as he asks," Will interjected. "I've never seen him this angry before." Will winked at Charlie.

There was another clatter from inside the trailer as something moved inside. Valerie realized there and then that the lock on the door wasn't working. Pete was moving something heavy away from the door, something he had been using to keep it shut.

A pale face peeked out from behind the door.

"I.. I'm Pete."

"Hi Pete," Valerie smiled. "We're looking for a Michael Shaw. We were told he often stays somewhere in this park. Do you know him?"

"No, sorry," he said. "I haven't been crashing here long. The few people who are here keep to themselves."

"Oh, I see," Valerie said. But her instinct was that he was lying. As part of her training, she always looked for little changes in a person's demeanor or face when a name was first mentioned. Pete's face became more flushed when she said Michael Shaw's name.

"I'm sorry I couldn't be more helpful."

"Michael Shaw," Will said, "has a record for being violent. You aren't scared of him, are you?"

Valerie liked Will's approach. She saw a flicker in Pete's eyelids when Will mentioned fear.

"How… How can I be afraid of someone I've never even heard of?" he asked.

"Okay, Pete," Valerie said. "Have you seen any other strange goings on around here? Anyone carrying a knife, for example, or having blood on them?"

"No," he said. "Everyone keeps to themselves around here. I don't know anyone. I'm thinking of moving on, anyway. This place gives me the creeps. Nothing but trouble."

"I thought you said you hadn't seen anything strange?" Charlie asked.

"I haven't *seen* anything strange," Pete replied, snarkily. "But I've heard things. People walking through the park at night. I have a roof here, but I think I preferred the streets where you were out in the open if anything happened."

"So, you'll be moving along?" Will asked.

"Yes," Pete answered. "Now, why don't you try one of the other trailers. There are three or four ex-bikers living over there. I've seen them. Maybe they know this Martin Shaw character."

"Michael," Valerie said, correcting him.

"Oh, yes, sorry. Michael."

"I guess there's nothing else," Valerie said.

"But…" Charlie began.

"No, Charlie, let's use our time more wisely. We can head back to the station after we've spoken to these ex-bikers and then see if we can find any other new leads." Valerie turned back to Pete. "Thank you for your time. Sorry for disturbing you."

"It's quite all right," said, closing the door.

Valerie walked away from the trailer and her two companions followed.

"Didn't you think he knew something?" Charlie asked.

"Absolutely," Valerie answered. "He knows Michael Shaw."

"When he said Martin instead of Michael," Will observed, "it seemed like he was trying to be a bit too clever to put us off."

"Yeah," Valerie said. "He knows… He knows…"

"We should put a stakeout on the trailer," Charlie advised. "Get another agent or someone from Boston PD to follow him."

"No need," Valerie said, confidently. "I saw a few tells in his expression. He *is* scared of Michael Shaw, but also devoutly loyal to him. If we hide over by those bushes and wait, it won't be long until he leaves his trailer to go find him. I'm convinced of it."

"A thermos would have been good," Will said as they trampled quietly through the undergrowth. "Some coffee is much needed."

They stood behind a large bush and Valerie was now contented. "He can't see us in here. And there are no street lights near us. Let's wait."

"I hope we're not waiting too long," Will said. "I bought these shoes in Italy and they aren't made for this kind of terrain. They're already wet."

Charlie lifted one foot up and tapped the steel toe caps on them. "American made." He grinned.

"Perhaps I'm just more cosmopolitan than you, dear Charlie," Will whispered jokingly. "I'll take you to a real shoe store when this is over."

"Maybe," Charlie whispered back. "I'd rather eat my shoes than wear what you have on."

"It's Etruscan leather," Will quipped. "It would taste delicious."

"Quiet down, boys," Valerie said. She knew when they were trying to avoid feeling afraid. But it wasn't the time for jokes any more. Something was happening.

Across the way from them, the door to Pete's trailer opened. He emerged sheepishly, looking around to see if the coast was clear.

He then moved quickly across the waste ground towards the eastern shadows. Valerie was afraid he would move in that direction. There was no lighting over there, and a thick wall of night hid that section of the park from prying eyes.

But nonetheless, they had to follow.

It was the only way for them to know if Pete would lead them to Michael Shaw, the violent criminal who Valerie felt was lurking nearby.

A man, if his records were to be believed, who was capable of anything, including brutal murder.

# CHAPTER FIFTEEN

Charlie was frustrated with Valerie.

They were moving as quickly and as quietly as they could across the darkness of the abandoned trailer park. Unable to use their flashlights, they were having to use the sound of Pete's footsteps to track him.

But Valerie suggested they were going off in the wrong direction.

"I'm telling you," she said, speaking low and whispered. "I saw him go off at a 40 degree angle towards that line of bushes over there."

"How could you see?" Charlie asked. "There are no street lights over there."

"I saw his outline."

"There are other people in the park," Will offered. "Could it have been someone else?"

"No, I'm... I'm sure," Valerie said, unconvincingly.

"But I can hear him up ahead," Charlie said.

He was used to Valerie listening to him when it came to his hearing. He'd always been able to track sounds from far away ever since he was a kid. It had come in handy during Afghanistan, and it had saved his life on more than one occasion while chasing fugitives for the FBI.

But Valerie was preoccupied. Charlie could sense that. She kept staring off to the side, looking at something. To Charlie, it felt as though she had seen *something* in the shadows, but she was hesitant.

He had noticed a strange part of Valerie's behavior recently. On more than one occasion, he had seen her turn suddenly as if responding to something that wasn't there.

He put it down to her being jumpy and stressed about her mom and sister being in psychiatric wards, but in this instance, it was leading her to a mistake. And in their line of work, a mistake could prove fatal. For everybody.

For the first time since the Criminal Psychopathy Unit had been up and running, Charlie felt like all three of them were off their A-game. And that could be disastrous.

"Val, please," he said in a hushed voice. "Pete is moving further away, we're going to lose him if we go over there."

"He's over there," she said, frustration in her voice and pointing in the other direction.

Charlie felt his own frustrations bubbling over. "Right, you two go that way, I'm going up ahead."

"Is that wise?" Will asked. "I thought we agreed not to split up?"

"Will's right," Valerie said. "We should stick together. I don't want to pull seniority, Charlie."

"Then don't." Charlie was surprised at his own words. While they were both agents, if it came down to a veto, Valerie was the lead agent on the team. This had never caused issues before. But on that piece of darkened waste ground, as their target moved further away, Charlie just *knew* Valerie was wrong. And it would cost them their only lead.

Valerie looked at Charlie. They glared at each other. For a moment, Charlie thought she *was* going to pull rank. But she tried to be more diplomatic than that. "Fine, go. Come on, Will."

Will reluctantly left with Valerie. Charlie watched them heading off to an old burned out car overgrown with weeds. His one solace in the confrontation with Valerie was that he at least knew *they* were safe. They were going away from the danger.

Charlie was moving straight towards it.

With his revolver drawn, he moved quietly over the ground. His footsteps were deadened by a walking technique his old sarge had taught him back at Kabul. It required concentration. The trick was to not move too quickly or softly.

A soft footstep would brush against the grass or move gravel. A quick footstep would do the same. No, Charlie was now moving more deliberately than that. Firm and slow footsteps were needed to minimize any noise.

In the darkness, it was very difficult to see. Thankfully, the moon was up above, peeking out from behind sporadic clouds. It gave Charlie enough illumination to see a short distance ahead.

As he moved, he listened. He would take a few steps and then stop, listen for the footsteps, and then move again. He repeated this over and over again.

The footsteps of the man he was chasing had suddenly changed direction. Instead of moving forward in a straight line, they were now moving quickly at a forty degree angle.

Charlie wasn't far behind now. He stepped and then saw why the man up ahead had changed direction. He was walking around a large pond. The water was stagnant. There was no breeze, but Charlie could smell the stench in the air as it clung to it. No doubt something was rotting in the water.

*An old water feature*, Charlie thought. He imagined what the trailer park had been like in its heyday. Children playing in the streets, grandparents sitting outside their trailers watching the sun go down. This was home for someone. Even now, in the darkness, the weeds, and the rust, it was still home to a few. People with nowhere else to go.

Charlie walked away from the pond. Up ahead of him, he could see the dim outline of Pete, the man they had questioned back at the trailer. He had lied to them, and Charlie was now under no illusion: He knew something about Michael Shaw.

*Are you running from or towards something?* That was the question on Charlie's lips. If Valerie and Will had been beside him, he would have asked their opinion. But they were off chasing Valerie's shadows.

Pulling out his cellphone, Charlie crouched down behind a bush and quickly texted Valerie. "He's up ahead from me. Following."

Putting the phone away, he continued behind the man. Now, he was getting closer. And as the gap reduced, the chance of Pete seeing or hearing him grew.

Charlie was trying to be patient. He remembered a game he and his brother Marvin used to play as kids. It was called One Man Hunt. Charlie remembered an occasion where Marvin had hid inside the trunk of an old car at a junkyard.

Even when they were kids, Charlie knew how to track. And a good thing, too. Marvin's footprints had led Charlie to where he was hiding. The trunk was closed and had jammed. And the car was going to be carted off by some of the guys working at the yard to be crushed.

One time of many where Marvin's recklessness had nearly proven fatal.

Charlie snapped back to his immediate situation. He was beginning to realize just how much his brother's appearance back home had affected him. Charlie always focused on the here and now, especially during a case. But that had changed. His brother was on his mind, and that wasn't going away any time soon.

The moon above poked momentarily through the clouds, lighting the area a little more. Charlie saw the outline of a large trailer. Out front of it was an old rowing boat that had rotted in the middle and was now in two pieces. The trailer itself wasn't doing much better.

Stopping by the boat and crouching down, Charlie watched as Pete reached the door of the trailer.

"Hey, Mike. We've… We've got a problem," Pete said, nervously looking around him.

"What is it, Jake?" a gruff voice groaned from inside.

*So Pete isn't your name. Nice to meet you, Jake*, Charlie thought, sarcastically.

"Christ, open up!" Jake said louder this time.

The door opened and Charlie grimaced at what he saw. He knew instinctively that it was Michael Shaw who was standing in the doorway. But the man was clearly on steroids. With his shirt off, he looked powerful and muscular.

Charlie was no slouch himself, but even an averagely built man could be difficult to subdue if he was fighting for his life. But someone on "the sauce" as some called it… That would be even more trying. Not only did it make a person stronger, but it also made them more aggressive. That was a combination Charlie didn't want to experience on his own with a guy pushing six-five.

"I'm busy!" the man stood, towering above Jake.

"Come back to bed," the voice of a woman said from inside the trailer.

"Oh, you've got company?" Jake sounding surprised. "You might want to…"

"Cut to the chase, Jake. What is it?"

"FBI are here," Jake said, his voice anxious. "They came to my trailer. They were looking for you."

Michael Shaw stepped out of the doorway. In the moonlight, his shaved head made him look every inch a thug. He walked over to Jake and grabbed him by the cuff of his coat.

"And what did you say to the FBI Jake?"

"Nothing!" Jake replied. "I swear!"

"You telling me the truth, my man?"

"I wouldn't lie, Mike. Not after what you did to me last time."

Michael Shaw let go of Jake and grinned. "Yeah. I believe you're not that stupid. Where are the feds now?"

"They said they were leaving, that they had to go regroup."

"You idiot!" Shaw pushed Jake to the ground. He fell with a thud through a bush.

"What did I do wrong?" Jake said, his voice wavering as if hurt from the fall.

"They made you think they were going. They probably followed you here!"

Michael Shaw looked out into the night. And that was when Charlie felt the man's stare fall on him. Now Charlie had no choice. He had to act, with or without Valerie and Will.

Charlie rushed forward, gun drawn.

"FBI! Hands up!"

Michael Shaw reached his hands up into the air. Jake stood up, too. Putting his hands in the air. But that only gave Shaw an opportunity He grabbed Jake, wrapped his arm around his throat from behind, and then used him as a shield.

"I swear I'll snap this bum's neck!" he yelled, pulling Jake back with him. He reached one hand into the doorway.

Charlie couldn't get a clean shot, but he instinctively knew what Shaw was doing. The man pulled a hand gun from the inside of the trailer's door frame and let off three shots.

They rang out, spraying up dirt and gravel from the ground as Charlie leaped behind the old rowing boat. A fourth shot splintered against the wood. The boat might not have been sea worthy, but the old girl sheltered Charlie long enough to crawl around to the other side of its broken hull.

Charlie waited. Another shot was fired, striking the hull where Shaw had last seen him hide. This was enough for Charlie to know that the shooter was unaware he had moved.

In one deft move, Charlie slid onto the ground out from behind the boat and let off two shots. One brought a scream. He'd hit Jake in the foot. The second struck Michael Shaw in the shin.

Shaw dropped Jake to the ground and limped off behind the trailer while Jake screamed holding his foot. Charlie stood up and gave chase.

"You shot my foot!" Jake cried out as Charlie passed.

"You'll live," said Charlie as he followed the limping footsteps of Michael Shaw into the shadows.

Passing between two more trailers, Charlie realized the danger ahead. He couldn't see where Shaw was, and he was heading into open ground with little cover. There was a silence in the park, but for the still crying Jake somewhere to the rear.

Shaw wasn't moving anymore. Instead, he was using the bleak night for cover. If Charlie had been able to, he would have used his flashlight, but that would have only telegraphed his position to the shooter.

The thought of his flashlight alerting Shaw to where he was gave Charlie an idea. But he would need to use his environment if it was to work.

Looking across the way, he saw a line of eight or nine trees to the east. Making it to them would be tricky. They were a relic from the past, years ago shepherding residents of the trailer park along the path which they lined. Now, standing like ominous guardians of the trailer park, they provided a life line. They provided cover.

Charlie headed for them.

As he did, he heard a gunshot whiz past his head. But Shaw wouldn't have realized that was what Charlie wanted. The muzzle flash lit up the angered face of Michael Shaw, and that gave away *his* position.

Charlie reached the trees, turned full tilt and squeezed the trigger of his revolver three times. Shaw let out a yelp as one of the bullets caught him in the shoulder.

But the man was unstoppable, he grabbed the bloodied wound, held his hand over it and shouted: "Is that all you got?"

Scanning the trailer park from the shadows of a large tree, Charlie watched as Shaw fired back. Each time, the muzzle flash moved with him as he ran in the opposite direction of Charlie's hiding place.

The last of four shots lit up the area around Shaw, revealing a large structure behind him. Charlie strained to hear. He just about made out the sound of feet rushing across a wooden floor.

"He's gone inside somewhere," Charlie said to himself.

Moving back across the ground away from the tree line, Charlie could feel his heart racing. He was out in the open, exposed. It was dangerous, but Charlie felt he had no other option. If he let Michael Shaw run, he could get away and kill more innocent women.

Charlie's feet padded the ground, and he ran as fast as he could, hoping the cloud cover above would obscure him from the moonlight.

As he ran, the structure he had seen lit up by Shaw's last muzzle flash finally came slowly into view. In the darkness, it was a grim rectangular outline, two stories high. In every way, it looked like an abandoned building out of some nightmarish slasher film.

Charlie reached its front. He strained his eyes to see that it was once some epicenter to the park. Either an administrative building or perhaps a store. But it had long since been abandoned.

Some windows were smashed, others boarded up. The front door was lying on the ground, completely removed from its hinges. Charlie stepped inside.

It smelled of damp. Near his feet, he could see a faded information board on the floor. But he couldn't read what was on it.

Ducking down next to an old counter, he listened.

But the building hid Shaw well. Creaks and groans from the structure surrounded him, the hallmarks of a building just waiting for time to crumble it into the ground. They were almost impossible to separate from the movement of a fugitive through its darkened rooms.

Charlie didn't dare put on his flashlight. He would have to use his senses as best he could.

It was difficult to step through the fallen pieces of wood and plaster on the floor without making noise. He just hoped he could keep his footsteps as quiet as possible. If the building's noises could protect Shaw, they could obscure Charlie, too.

He looked through a blackened doorway. In the gloom, he could see flakes of white paint blistering off the frame like wrinkles. Gun in hand, he drew close to see what was inside.

Something scuttled across the floor, moving several pieces of debris. Instinctively, Charlie looped his finger through the trigger of his revolver, but he was able to seize himself in the last moment and stop himself from firing.

Eyes gleamed in a ray of moonlight that poked down through a hole in the roof above.

*Rats*, he thought to himself. He didn't want to deal with that. The idea of a swarm of them crawling up his legs and body was enough to make his stomach turn. But he still had to check the room, regardless.

Going further in, he saw that it was some sort of old storage room, filled with broken bottles and lines for old refrigerator units. Someone had torn the walls open and pulled out all of the copper piping, no doubt to sell it.

A door to the rear of the room was blocked by a section of the ceiling that had caved in, but another doorway led to a small section with some stairs at the end of it.

He crept along the corridor, perspiration beading on his brow.

Reaching the foot of the staircase, Charlie wondered if the thing could take his weight. Looking closely, he could see a layer of dust on a few of the steps. It had been disturbed recently. A glance to a few steps above and there he saw some drops of blood.

*He's upstairs*, Charlie thought.

Heading up the stairs, he kept his gun out in front of him, half expecting to see Shaw at the top waiting to ambush him. But all that met him was an empty doorway.

The level above was even more rotten than the one below. But now there was more light, as sections of the decayed roof let in shafts of moonlight.

Charlie reckoned the cloud cover had cleared. Peering around, he was unsure where to step. That was when he glanced down through a big opening to the ground floor.

Eyes stared up at him again.

But this time, those eyes had a human face.

"Die, pig!" the man below screamed.

Two muzzle flashes lit up the area as Charlie dived behind an old support beam. The bullets smashed into damp plaster near his head.

Then, Charlie heard something else. A click.

*His weapon's jammed. Misfire!*

Rushing out from behind the support beam, Charlie rushed to the edge of the gaping hole.

"Freeze! Put down your weapon."

But Shaw didn't stop. He turned and ran, pulling at the gun in his hand as he moved.

Charlie had only one chance before man reloaded his gun and was out of sight. There was no time to descend the stairs or think about how dangerous his next move was.

He could only commit without fear.

He leaped off the floor, angling his body as it moved upwards and then gravity took over. He plunged down through the hole to the darkness below, reaching out with his elbow and bringing it down firmly on Shaw's back.

Shaw let out a scream and Charlie thumped to the ground. He looked up, the wind knocked out of him, and saw Michael Shaw wriggling on the ground holding his arm.

"You broke my arm! You broke my arm!" he shouted repeatedly.

Charlie was dazed. He could hardly breathe from the impact on the floor.

Then a moment. A stare between them. Both men could see their guns sitting on the floor between them.

Shaw angrily rolled over and reached for one of them, but Charlie was too far away.

As Shaw lifted the gun and pointed it at Charlie, a swift kick came from the darkness. The foot caught Shaw's hand, thumping the gun out of his grip.

Charlie was relieved. Standing above him was Agent Valerie Law. And she had just saved his life.

# CHAPTER SIXTEEN

Valerie had reached the point where coffee no longer helped. It only made her more jittery. It only increased her anxiety. It did not, unfortunately, keep her more awake.

A wave of tiredness was cascading over her.

And yet she kept drinking coffee into the small hours of the night in the hopes that it would quell her exhaustion.

It had been a *very* long day.

She, Will, and a bruised but recovered Charlie, were waiting in the interview room of Balenthaul Police Department back on the south side of Boston. The same fluorescent lights above that were used throughout the building bathed the small room in a harsh light. The walls, a specific off-white, gave a green hue to proceedings.

The bolted down metal table in front of the three investigators and the empty chair accompanying it reminded Valerie of a hundred different police interview rooms. Each one melted into another in her memory.

She just hoped that the chair would soon be filled with a suspect. She hoped he was the killer, so that she could bring an end to the death stalking Boston.

They had caught Michael Shaw.

A search of the park had revealed his prints all over several other trailers, some of them used to make drugs. And Bill had said he might be the murderer based on his mug shot. But it was his use of the shadows in the trailer park that piqued Valerie's interest the most. Very similar to how the killer maneuvered. She knew it was now a very real possibility that they had caught their man.

Will looked at his watch.

"You know, Will," said Charlie. "There's a clock up there."

"I'm not sure I trust it," Will said. "This is a precision piece of timekeeping. Swiss made. My old professor back at Harvard gave me it."

"And what does it say?" Valerie asked, looking at a paper file in front of her.

Will grumbled under his breath. "It says it's about the same time as the clock."

"I'm glad we got that settled," Charlie said, sarcastically. "To be fair, it does feel like time is moving slower in here." He winced slightly, holding his side, and shifting his weight on his chair to get comfortable.

"How are your ribs?" Valerie asked.

"Fine," he said. "I feel like they take a battering on every case now. Probably should wear body armor."

"Come on..." Valerie sighed, looking at the clock and feeling the weight of her eyelids.

The clock's face read 2:32AM, and with each passing minute she lost hope that she'd be getting any sleep that night.

Finally, the door opened. In stepped detective Monaghan looking as disheveled as ever and, if possible, even more caffeinated than Valerie. He led the towering, limping figure of Michael Shaw into the room. The man was cuffed, and his left arm in plaster. He was clearly struggling to put weight on the leg where he'd taken a bullet, but Valerie knew a man like that wouldn't want to show too much weakness. Black and blue inked tattoos climbed his muscular arms like ivy.

"I'm glad you could finally join us, Mr. Shaw," Charlie said.

"Maybe if you hadn't shot me," said Shaw, "I wouldn't have taken so long." He looked at the cuffs around his wrists as Monaghan sat him down in front of Valerie. "You're lucky I have these on. I'd tear you a new one."

"You'd try," said Charlie.

"Mr. Shaw," Valerie said. "Do you know why we were at the trailer park tonight?"

"Who knows?" he answered, grinning.

"I might be able to help you with that," Monaghan said, still standing. "We found a small meth lab tucked away in the corner of the trailer park."

Shaw's grin turned to anger. "I don't know nothing about that!"

"That's strange," offered Monaghan, scratching his messy hair. "Because we found your finger prints all over the place. You want that lawyer now?"

Valerie was glad Monaghan was there to turn the screw.

"I trust lawyer scum even less than pigs like you," Shaw seethed. "I don't need nothin'."

90

"In that case," Will added. "Tell us, why do you hate women so much?"

Shaw seemed surprised at the direct question. Like a child who'd had his hand caught in the cookie jar and thought no one would notice.

"What's that supposed to mean?"

Will pointed to one of the tattoos on his arm. "Your tattoos give away more about you than you know. This one here in particular. A woman with a tentacle wrapped around her. Why did you choose that one?"

Shaw shrugged his shoulders. "I dunno. Seemed cool."

Will took off his glasses and glared across the table. "The tentacle constrains the woman. She's reaching up with her arm, helpless. The beast is pulling her down to the abyss. And look at the next tattoo above it. A grinning skull."

"So?" Shaw said, sounding defensive. "They're just ink."

"I think you want to control women," Will said. "And if you can't, well, then they might as well dance with death, no?"

Shaw tensed up for a moment. Valerie saw a vein running down from his jaw to his neck pulse as he clenched down on his teeth. She suspected he was on steroids. But he seemed too smart to take Will's bait. He leaned back in his chair, relaxed, and said: "Just charge me, if you're gonna charge me. I want to go to my nice new cozy cell and have a cat nap. Then, I'll be out by morning."

"We can place you in that meth lab, Shaw," Monaghan said.

"So, my fingerprints might be in there," he said. "Maybe I'm just an addict."

"Or maybe you're making the stuff in there to sell it?" said Monaghan.

"You couldn't prove that even if it was true, pig."

Something buzzed momentarily in the light above. Valerie felt as though the light subtly flickered, but no one else noticed. The dread was starting. She needed sleep to keep her paranoid mind at bay.

"We're not interested in the meth lab, for now at least," Charlie said. "We're interested in the two young women who've been cut up in Boston this week."

Shaw's grin fell away. He leaned forward. "Now wait a second… I've done a lot of bad stuff in my time, but cutting up girls ain't one of them."

"You clearly show an affinity with controlling women, Mr. Shaw," Will added.

"That's… That's not the same as killing, is it?"

"No," said Will. "But you seem to enjoy controlling women. That can easily lead to ultimate control, taking their lives."

"Hold on! What are you trying to pin on me?"

"What about the woman in your trailer?" Charlie said, grimly. "Sounds like you had influence over her. Is she into meth? Is that how you control women?"

Shaw gritted his teeth and then took a deep breath. He leaned back in his seat and grinned mischievously. "The women don't come to me for the meth. You married, Carlson? How about I visit your wife and you can see why the women like me."

Charlie stood up as quick as lightning and lurched across the table to grab Shaw. Valerie was quick to the task, as were Monaghan and Will. Between the three of them, they managed to pull Charlie away from the prisoner and towards the door.

"Charlie, think this through!" Will said, his voice booming louder than Valerie was used to.

"He's a scumbag, Agent Carlson," said Monaghan, "but let's not ruin any case we have against him by taking his bait, okay?"

Charlie eyeballed Shaw, who was still grinning at him from his seat.

Closing his eyes for a moment, Charlie's breathing slowed down. He opened his eyes, nodded, and then said: "I think I should take a breather."

"I'll come with you," said Valerie, worried for her partner.

Valerie, Will, and Charlie left the room, closing the door behind them as they entered the stark corridor outside.

"Charlie, that's not like you," Valerie said in a low voice.

Shaking his head, Charlie took a moment to answer. "I'm sorry. The guy is getting to me. This whole thing is."

"It's not like you to bring stresses into the job, Charlie," Will said, softly. "Maybe you need some time off to deal with the situation with your brother back home."

"No," Charlie said, fixing his jacket. "It's fine. I'm fine. I'm sorry."

"You know we're here if…" Valerie said.

Charlie cut her off, but did so gently: "No, Val. It's okay. I had a slip in there. But I've got my head together."

Footsteps now sounded in the corridor. Valerie turned and looked down the hall to see Bill Creed, the homeless man who had witnessed the second murder, walking, accompanied by a police officer.

"Ah, that's good," Valerie said, approaching.

"Hi, Agent Law," Bill said, sheepishly.

"Are they treating you okay, Bill?" Will asked.

"Sure thing," said Bill. "I'll be giving a rave review." He smiled revealing yellowed teeth.

"The reason I asked for you," Valerie said, "is that we have a suspect in that room. And we think he might be the killer. Would you be willing to ID him?"

"Ugh," Bill said, seeming frightened. "I'm not sure."

Valerie understood his fears. If the homeless people she'd already spoken to were a measure of anxiety on the streets, Bill was afraid somehow the killer would find him.

"It's anonymous," Will said, gently. "Perhaps we could informally look before we sort out a lineup?"

"That's an idea," Charlie said.

"If you come into this room," Valerie suggested, pointing to the door next to the interview room, "we have a two-way mirror set up."

"He won't see me?" Bill asked, his voice still hesitant.

"No," Valerie answered. "And if he is the killer, we can lock him away for a long time and make sure he never hurts anyone else."

Bill took a moment as if mulling it over. "Okay," he said. "I'll do it."

"Thank you," said Will.

"Good man," added Charlie.

Valerie opened the door to the next room and they went inside. The interior was dark, but the wall was transparent, a looking glass into where Shaw and Monaghan now sat.

Michael Shaw was tapping his fingers on the table, and Monaghan looked as though he would fall asleep if someone didn't go in and relieve him soon.

"Take a good look, Bill," Will said. "If you can think about the…"

"It's not him," Bill said, plainly.

Valerie felt her heart sink. "Are you sure?"

"Yes," Bill answered.

"How sure?"

"100%," he said, confidently. "I'd never forget the shape of the guy in the shadows. He was tall and lean. This man is too muscular. The killer wasn't so bulky. He moved like an athlete, not someone on 'roids."

"Let's not be too hasty, Bill," Charlie said. Valerie could hear a slight desperation in his voice. He'd just gone through a lot to bring the prisoner in. For him to not be the killer was more than disheartening.

"I'm sorry, everyone," Bill said, sounding hurt that he couldn't help more.

Will patted him on the shoulder. "It's okay, Bill. If you had said yes and he hadn't been the killer, we would have stopped looking for the real one. That would have given him another opportunity to kill. You've been a huge help letting us cross this one off our list of suspects."

"List?" Valerie said out loud, sounding incredulous.

Will looked back, his eyes gently persuading Valerie to support the statement.

"Oh, right," said Valerie. "The list of suspects. Yes, Mr. Creed. You've been a huge help."

Valerie caught Charlie's expression. It was a defeated one.

They were exhausted. After everything they had been through, they were no closer to catching the killer. At least, if Bill Creed was right.

Valerie knew Michael Shaw would be charged with resisting arrest, possessing an illegal firearm, and, if Monaghan could make it stick, running a meth lab. In any other case, that would have been a result to be proud of. But not this one. Not when the killer was on the loose.

A killer hell bent on escalation at a frightening rate.

Looking at Monaghan on the other side of the glass, his eyes weary, his head being propped up on the table by his hands, she knew they all would need some sleep.

They had to come back stronger tomorrow. And hope beyond hope that they didn't wake to the news of another brutal murder.

But in Valerie's heart of hearts, she fully expected bad news the next morning, when the sun would rise on more death and carnage.

# CHAPTER SEVENTEEN

Valerie thought the lobby to the Chambers Hotel was more like a chamber of horror. Deep red carpets and curtains encircled the space, polished stone floors carrying decades of chips and cracks, and a rather unsavory looking painting of the hotel itself above the reception, all gave the impression of a place that feigned its welcome.

But Valerie didn't much care. It was nearly four in the morning, and she just wanted the key to her room.

Will stared at the sickly looking man behind the reception desk. "Surely you have more than two rooms?"

"I'm afraid not," the man at the reception said. "We double booked. I'm sorry."

"Looks like we're bunking," Charlie said to Will.

Will let out a sigh. "All right. But just so you know, I like to snuggle."

Charlie let out a boisterous laugh. His spirits had improved since the altercation with Michael Shaw. Valerie reckoned he had realized he'd overstepped the mark and was doing his best to pull himself out of his worries.

She hoped it would work.

"I'll take one of the rooms," Valerie said. The receptionist handed her the key to room 16.

Valerie turned to her friends. "Get some rest, guys. Oh, and Will, I've shared a room with Charlie before. He snores. A quick pillow over the face usually does the trick."

"Good night, Val," said Charlie. Then Will repeated the sentiment.

"Good night, guys."

Valerie left the lobby and headed up the stairs with her suitcase. It thudded against the well-trodden carpets of the hotel. Reaching a long hallway that looked as anonymous as the others in the building, she finally found her room.

Inside, she took little notice of the peeling wallpaper and musty smell. Sleep was what she needed. Sleep was what she yearned for.

Taking off her clothes, she slid underneath the cold blanket, switched off the light, and closed her eyes.

Sleep should have come easily. But it did not. Instead, a tsunami that had been held up by the case, now unleashed in her mind.

Thoughts slowly peeled away. She thought of her dad refusing the DNA test. She thought of her mom and sister, straightjackets and all, and, finally, she thought of Tom and the engagement.

Turning onto her side, she tried an old technique. She counted her breaths. But it didn't help. Her life was swirling around her head.

And that was when she heard the noise from the bathroom.

It sounded like something familiar. The sound a naked foot makes as it steps onto cold tiles.

*I didn't check the bathroom*, Valerie thought as she opened her eyes.

Another sound. Another footstep on the tiles.

Valerie looked up towards the closed door of the bathroom. She felt the jolt of adrenaline passing through her veins. Her breathing began to shake slightly.

Looking over, she saw that she had left her jacket on the back of a chair. Her revolver was in its holster inside of it.

*Stupid*, she thought. But she had been so tired, she had forgot to put her firearm in the drawer next to the bed.

Another sound. The subtlest of movements.

*Who is in there?* She thought.

Valerie didn't want to give away that she was reacting to the sound. She had to move quietly, though quickly, and hope that she could reach her gun before whoever was in the bathroom confronted her.

Lifting the blanket quietly, she put her feet on the hotel room floor. The floorboards creaked as she shifted her weight.

That creak went straight through Valerie's nerves like an ice pick. She was sure she heard the person in the bathroom move and pick something up. In her mind it was a weapon. It clinked slightly as though it had been resting in a sink.

Valerie kept her eyes trained on the door. She moved to the bottom of the bed, expecting the door to be flung open with anger, and some large, hulking individual with a grudge to rush through the doorway at her.

But the door remained closed.

She reached her jacket on the back of the chair and pulled the revolver from it. Now she felt a modicum of control. Though the fears in her mind were still rampant. For all she knew, the individual in the bathroom was armed with a gun.

*Is it the killer?* she thought.

But that didn't make sense to Valerie. She had only just been given the room. How would the killer have known which room she was in?

Then another thought occurred to her. *What if the receptionist was in on it?*

They had called ahead earlier in the day. They knew the FBI agents were staying there. It was in the local area. Could they have been so unlucky as to have booked in a place with the killer or an accomplice?

Valerie's tired mind was frazzled. She knew it was such an unlikely turn of events. All she *was* sure of, was that someone was in the bathroom when they shouldn't have been.

She steadied herself and moved across the floor towards the bathroom door. From that vantage point, she noticed that the door wasn't locked. It was very slightly ajar.

Through the slimmest of gaps, she could see only gray outlines.

*The light is off,* she thought. *They're hiding in the darkness.*

Valerie pointed her gun at the door. "I'm armed and pointing a gun at the door," she finally said. "I'm also an FBI agent, so you picked the wrong room to hide in. Come out with your hands up."

Straining to listen, Valerie then heard something that turned her blood cold. A laugh. It was a distant, short one, but she was certain it came from behind the door.

She was sure of one other thing. The laugh belonged to her mother.

In a moment of abject horror, Valerie kicked at the door. It swung open. She smacked the light switch with her hand, never taking her eyes and aim from the doorway.

The light flickered on.

The bathroom was empty.

Valerie checked behind the door. No one was there.

Her hands were shaking.

*It's happening. The illness is coming.*

Valerie had chased down some of the most violent killers in the world. But as she slipped back into bed, tears streaming down her cheeks, there was only one fear that occupied her thoughts.

The fear that she was finally losing her mind.

# CHAPTER EIGHTEEN

The killer felt the weight of the manhole cover above him. He pushed up with force and the metal slid off, revealing a cold night and a harsh Boston street above.

Pulling himself up, he breathed the air. It made him feel alive as he stood up and replaced the cover.

A smile washed over his face as he realized he was in the right place.

"Ellison Street," he said to himself, closing his eyes.

Somewhere in the distance, the traffic moved, car wheels splashing through murky puddles taking drivers and passengers alike to unknown places.

The sounds were just as they had been in the past. He could smell the rain entering the gutters. The smell was the same, too. Memories sparked and flowed through his mind.

A feeling of well-being washed over him as he stood on the street.

*Yes, this is a special place*, he thought to himself.

In his mind he heard the sound of underprivileged children playing together well past their bedtimes. They ran around. The night was theirs. The world was theirs. It was good to be alive.

And now he was waiting. Waiting for that special person to arrive in his memory. To feel that love again. That sense of security.

"Are you okay?" a voice said in front of him. But it was not one from his memory.

The killer opened his eyes and saw a man in his fifties wearing a white apron in front of him.

"Are you okay?" he repeated.

Anger began to swell inside.

"Leave me alone," the killer offered. It was the only warning he would give.

He closed his eyes again and tried to get back to that memory. The sights. The sounds. The smells. The people.

"I was watching you from our window over there," the man in the white apron said. "My name's Gareth. I run a homeless drop-in shelter.

We're 24/7. You look like you've been caught in the rain. You could come in and have some food if you like, get warm."

The killer was furious. He opened his eyes and considered the man.

"I'm not one of them," the killer said.

"Oh," the man replied. "I just saw you with your eyes closed out here. You know you're standing on a road? It could be dangerous." He smiled. "Homeless or not, why don't you come inside and get out of this cold wet night?"

The memory was gone now. The killer couldn't find it anymore. His peace had been broken. Broken by another do-gooder. Another freak who didn't know when to mind his own business.

"Do you like talking to strangers?" the killer asked.

The man seemed unnerved by this. He was still smiling, but his eyes were not jovial. He looked frightened.

"I asked you a question," the killer repeated. "Do *you* like talking to strangers?"

"Well, I was just trying to help and thought…"

"You think, too much, my friend," the killer said. "Sometimes, it's best to mind your own business. You took something from me… A memory… You've broken it… And now I can't find it…"

The man in the white apron started to back away.

"I'm sorry, I'll leave you alone."

"Thank you," said the killer.

Then then man in the white apron turned around to walk back to the drop-in shelter.

And that was when the killer lunged forward, wrapped his hands around his head and throat, and slit him open from ear to ear.

"Now you won't be bothering anyone," the killer whispered into the man's ear.

He dropped him to the ground like a bag of garbage, pulled up the manhole cover, and then disappeared back beneath the rainy streets of Boston.

Rain that now mixed with blood from another victim, and another life cut short.

# CHAPTER NINETEEN

Valerie felt the hands of the killer on her. They were strong, the fingers of her assailant wrapped around her shoulders as the man shook her.

She opened her eyes. Terror beckoned. She could feel a cold sweat washing over her body. She screamed as she flailed for her gun at the side of her bed, the man on top of her.

Then a second pair of hands reached, grabbing her wrist and stopping her from getting to her gun.

Valerie let out an almighty scream.

"Val! Val!" a familiar voice yelled.

She turned her head and looked up.

Two figures slowly came into view in the low light. It was Charlie and Will. Charlie was holding her by the shoulders, and Will was holding her wrist.

"My God…" she said.

Charlie let go and stepped back. Valerie pulled herself up on the dingy hotel room bed and wiped the sweat from her face.

Will sat down beside her on the bed and patted her hand. He was being gentle, but his eyes were filled with concern.

"What… What happened?" Valerie asked, trying to get her heart rate under control.

"Charlie and I tried knocking," Will said.

"We heard you scream," Charlie added, looking at Valerie with the same expression as Will.

"I must have been having a dream," was all Valerie could say, still disorientated as her mind woke up.

"We thought you were in trouble, so I kicked the door in," Charlie explained, pointing to the hotel room door and its busted lock.

Valerie could hear some movement out in the hallway. Charlie walked over to the door, stuck his head out and brandished his FBI badge.

"It's okay, folks. FBI business. Everything is okay, now."

He returned to the room, and the sound of the concerned hotel patrons in the hallway diminished as room doors closed.

Will was staring at Valerie intently.

"I'm sorry," she said. "I was just having a bad dream."

"Valerie," he said, softly. "That was no dream."

"Okay, a nightmare, then."

"Worst nightmare I've seen," said Charlie. "And I have kids."

"That was a classic night terror," Will said.

"I thought only children had those?" asked Charlie.

"Thanks," Valerie said sarcastically. "Nice to know I'm still young at heart."

"Night terrors can come at any age," Will continued, clearly not in the mood to be light-hearted about it. "Your eyes were open, you were outright hallucinating during the episode."

Valerie's thoughts turned to what she had heard in the bathroom before going to sleep. The hallucination of hearing her mother laughing.

But the night terror, this was something just as disturbing. Valerie knew that several psychiatric illnesses were accompanied by such episodes. In fact, they were often a precursor to a much more frightening, downward spiral.

"I'm sorry if I frightened you," Valerie said to her friends. "I…"

"You don't need to explain us," Charlie said, getting a bottle of water from the room refrigerator and handing it to Valerie. "I just need to know two things, Val."

"And they are?"

"Are you okay? And do you feel up to continuing on the case?"

Valerie felt a surge of defensive frustration swell up. She opened the bottle of water and took a slug, hoping to stop herself from saying something rash.

But it didn't.

"Do I ask you if you're fit to serve considering what's going on with your brother?"

"That's a little different…"

"Is it?" Valerie said. "And Will has been clearly affected by something he hasn't shared yet. Something connected to the homeless population in Boston. Do I question his ability to get things right?"

Will let go of Valerie's hand. He sighed. "Let's not go down the road of picking each other apart. We all have baggage. If we stick together, we can help each other carry it."

"I don't have baggage," Valerie said, shaking her head. "But it feels like I have two partners who don't quite trust me anymore."

"Trust's got nothing to do with it, Val," Charlie said. "You nearly grabbed your gun. You'd have gotten to it, too, if Will hadn't grabbed your wrist."

"I'm sorry," Valerie said. "Would it make you feel better if one of you kept my firearm at night?"

"I'm not saying we need to do that," Charlie sighed. "But I just want to know you're okay. You've been off, lately."

"We all have," Valerie struck back.

"True," said Will. "Charlie, would you give us a moment, please?"

Charlie shrugged his shoulders. "Sure." He left the room.

Will turned back to Valerie. "Valerie, I want to suggest something to you. And I say this as a friend, and as a trained professional. I think you should consider getting a therapist to help you through some of your problems. I know a tremendous therapist who could help."

"No thanks," said Valerie. "I'd rather just get on with things."

"Please think it over," Will suggested. "Talking with someone will help; it's helped me, you know."

Valerie felt shocked. She had no idea Will had needed any therapy before.

"Don't look so shocked," he said, smiling. "There has been more than one time in my life when I've needed to speak with a therapist. Putting things into context, exploring the trauma, these are pivotal to being happy. And all I want is to see *you* happy, Valerie. I'm afraid if you keep whatever is going on inside of you, it will eat you up."

Valerie felt herself calming. Will's words were always filled with care. She held his hand for a moment.

"You're an amazing friend, Will," she said. "I'll think about it, okay? That's all I can say right now."

Will nodded. "Do you feel up to…"

"I'll be fine, but give a girl some privacy to get dressed," Valerie said, laughing.

And that was when she finally saw the clock on the wall.

*6:20AM.*

"Why are you guys up so early?" Valerie asked.

Will looked at Valerie with a bleak look of sadness in his eyes.

"Valerie… There's been another murder… And it's not what we thought…"

# CHAPTER TWENTY

Valerie, Will, and Charlie looked down at the body on the road as the early morning rain soaked them all.

Detective Monaghan had pulled the rain sheet away to let them look at victim number three.

What she saw made no sense to her. It was a man in his fifties. His throat had been slit from ear to ear, and he had been left to bleed out on the street during the night.

"This doesn't make sense," she said almost under her breath.

"What doesn't?" asked Monaghan, looking so rough Valerie wondered if he'd been up drinking all night.

"The first two victims were women," Will said.

"And both in their twenties," added Charlie.

"This man is in his fifties," Valerie explained. "It completely breaks any possible victim profile. But the wounds are almost identical to the others. It has to be our killer who did this."

"Most of the local newspapers and channels have been advising young women to be careful," Monaghan sighed. "And now this. It doesn't exactly make us look good."

"What's the victim's name?" asked Valerie.

"Gareth Kowalski," Monaghan said. "He volunteered with a homeless drop-in center over there."

Valerie followed where Monaghan was pointing with his hand. Across the road, an old café was serving soup and sandwiches to several homeless people.

"Did anyone see what happened?" asked Charlie, wiping the rain from his face.

"No," answered Monaghan, his voice as grim as the weather. "Not a soul. He came out here, and it's as if the killer struck and just upped and vanished."

"Any security cam footage?" Will inquired.

Monaghan shook his head. "Again, nothing. And there is a camera at the end of this street. But no one came by around the time of death."

Valerie's thoughts raced. She closed her eyes to steady them for a moment.

*Think, think, think.*

A vision came to her. The subway where the first victim was murdered. The open hatch.

Valerie opened her eyes and started scanning around on the ground. She watched as the rain cascaded down the street, moving at a slight incline. Almost in a daze, she started to follow it.

"Valerie?" asked Will.

But she barely heard him. The sound of the rain drowned her thoughts. It drowned out the world. It was just her and the water.

Her feet splashed in the thin veneer of liquid covering the hard road surface as she moved. She remembered a rainy day as a child, chasing the water down a lonely street, gleefully. Watching as it moved off to the drains.

She remembered wondering what was down there beneath.

The water moved, and Valerie moved with it, until she stopped. In front of her was a brown, rusted manhole cover.

Leaning over, she looked at it. A crack in the side was letting the water drip down within. She reached into the crack, big enough for her fingers, and pulled with all her might.

The cover moved. It groaned. It relented.

Valerie stared into the black hole she had uncovered. Deep into the tunnels and sewers of Boston.

*You're down there somewhere*, she thought. *But why the tunnels? And why come up here?*

She stood again and looked at the area. She wondered if it had some meaning for the killer. Some importance.

The others soon caught up and surrounded the hole, looking down inside.

"He came up from in there," Valerie said, her voice mingling with the sound of rain spattering against the concrete around them. "That's why the security cam didn't see him."

"Maybe he hid in one of these buildings," Monaghan offered as an alternative. "He could have moved through them and come out the other side. I mean, that's better than a sewer, isn't it?"

Valerie shook her head. "No, Detective Monaghan. This killer moves with the tunnels of Boston. He knows them well."

"We can't police them" Monaghan sighed. "There are thousands of these things all 0ver the city."

"Maybe he knows that," said Charlie. "Could he be a civil engineer or work in the sewers? That would explain why he knows them so well."

"It's possible," said Will. "But I'm inclined to think he's still homeless. All three victims have been murdered somewhere in relation to the Boston homeless community."

"I've heard of guys killing homeless people," Monaghan said. "Someone who can't stand to look at them."

"Probably because they see their own wretchedness," Valerie mused. "But I don't think that's what we're dealing with here. All three victims have been where homeless people hang out, but none of them have been homeless themselves."

"Gareth Kowalski worked with them," Charlie said.

"We can't overlook the homeless connection," explained Will. "It seems unlikely to be a coincidence that the killer murdered someone in an alleyway where homeless people sleep, and then killed outside of a homeless shelter. There must be a connection."

"But I've no idea what that might be," Valerie said. "Do we alert reporters that he's using the tunnels around the city to move about?"

"I see no point; it might just cause panic," Charlie said.

"It's worth thinking about," Monaghan suggested. "I mean, someone might have seen this scumbag climbing in and out of a sewer where he lives or something."

Valerie looked up to the sky and let the rain wash over her face. She turned and then looked at the rain sheet covering the body back along the street.

Beyond that, she saw a woman in a similar white apron to the victim, standing outside of the drop-in center smoking a cigarette and looking on in disbelief at the body on the ground.

Valerie walked passed the deceased and over to the woman.

"Hello," she said. "I'm Agent Law with the FBI. Did you know the deceased?"

"Kind of," she said, taking a long drag on her cigarette. "We both volunteered here. Nice guy, but I'd only been on a shift with him a couple of times. Still, it's terrible."

"I know, I'm sorry," Valerie said sympathetically. "Were you working when…"

"Hell no," the woman said. "I just came here an hour ago to start my shift. I came to all of this. I tell you, makes me wonder if I should be doing this at all. It ain't safe."

"Do you know of anyone who visits the drop-in center who seems violent?"

"A few, but no one this bad. I mean, most of the people who come here are just confused and have mental health problems. They ain't violent. Not unless you push them over the edge. I doubt Gareth did that to anyone, from what I know of him. He always seemed so kind."

"What do you do if someone is threatening or difficult?" Valerie asked.

"We get the cops involved or the social services," she replied. "But we look after the volunteers... At least we did. If someone gets too pushy or disrespectful, they get banned from coming in, at least for a while."

Valerie looked around her. "Do you know anywhere around here where some of the people at the center might go? The ones who get banned?"

The woman seemed to hesitate for a moment, like she was wary.

"Anything you can tell me will help find Gareth's killer," Valerie said, nudging the woman closer to divulging information.

"You gotta make sure you don't tell anyone," she said. "We build up trust with the local community, and sometimes you get info, you know?"

"What kind of information?"

"About places... Places where someone on the street can go and get dry. Maybe even sleep. But places where they technically shouldn't be."

Valerie nodded, but she realized she was going to have to fish the exact information out of the woman. "So, there's somewhere nearby where homeless people stay that's unofficial? And you think that if someone couldn't use this drop-in center..."

"They'd go there," the woman said. "It's not a nice place. But there are people there who can get things they need. They can get them food. Clothes. Unfortunately drugs and alcohol as well."

"Would you be willing to tell me where?" Valerie asked in hope.

"Yeah," the woman said. "But you gotta promise me you won't tell a soul I sent you there. I'd lose trust from a lot of the folks out here. And then they might not come here anymore. Believe me, the last thing I wanna do is force anyone away from a legit place like here that can help."

"You have my word," Valerie said.

"Okay," the woman looked around as if making sure no one else was watching. She pointed down the street away from the crime scene. "You want to take the first left, then your second right. Keep walking until you see an old wholesalers that's closed down. The windows are boarded up. Then, if you have to, go into the basement."

"The basement?" Valerie asked.

"They sleep underground next to some old heating pipes they still got going," she said. "There's some old tunnels or something down there. At least, that's what I hear. You ain't catching me down there. Even if I was homeless."

"Thank you for all of your help," Valerie said, elated.

This was it.

Valerie rushed back over to Will and Charlie.

"I've got a great lead," she said.

"Care to share?" Detective Monaghan said, overhearing.

"There's a place near here where homeless people sometimes take shelter," Valerie explained. "It sounds like it might be some sort of black market where they can get shelter and drugs. If someone knew the drop-in center but had been turned away for threatening behavior, one of the volunteers told me they might go there. And…"

"Why do I get a feeling I'm not going to like this?" Will said.

"It's underground," Valerie said quietly.

"So, if someone from the homeless community is using sewers and other tunnels…" Charlie thought out loud.

"Then this sounds like the perfect place for them to hide out and gain access," Valerie said.

"So what now?" asked Will.

Valerie turned and looked back at the body under the sheet. She had to find this killer.

"We go underground."

# CHAPTER TWENTY ONE

Valerie looked at the outside of the boarded up building with dread. Will, Charlie, and Detective Monaghan stood beside her. To any outsider like her, it appeared to be as abandoned as any she had seen in that part of the city.

But now that she knew to give it more than passing attention, there were telltale signs this was not the case. It held secrets or at least, the people within did.

A couple of homeless people were hanging around the doorway to the building, and although the door looked boarded over, to Valerie's eyes, the individuals seemed like guards.

Further along the front of the sandstone building, Valerie noticed a man in a long brown coat handing something to another man.

"Drugs," Valerie said quietly to the group. "That man outside is a pusher."

"I can have this building searched inch by inch within the hour," Monaghan offered.

"I appreciate that, Detective," said Valerie.

"Why do I get the feeling you're not taking him up on his offer?" Will asked.

"Because it would blow our chances," Charlie said. "If there are tunnels under that building leading to other parts of the sewer infrastructure, the killer could just disappear easily the second we entered the building."

"Agreed," said Valerie, still looking across the street to the building.

"I'll go in and scout around, ask a few questions," Charlie suggested.

Valerie ran her hand through her hair and fixed the hair pin that held it up. "No, Charlie. I think you've done enough chasing in the dark. It's my turn. Besides, you're still carrying an injury from the fight with Shaw at the trailer park."

Will stepped forward. "Valerie, I don't like the idea of you going in there by yourself."

Smiling back at Will, she tried to set his mind at ease. "I'll have my phone."

"And get a clean reception underground?" Will prodded.

"I don't want to shake the hornet's nest just yet," she explained. "We don't even know if the killer is in there or anyone will have information about him."

"I still think you should let the PD go in, Agent Law," said Monaghan.

"Maybe later," she said. "But a sure way to make someone clam up is using too much force. Let's tread softly at first. Wish me luck."

"I don't like this, Val," Charlie complained.

"That's why you're a good partner," said Valerie. "If you don't hear from me in thirty minutes, send in the cavalry."

Charlie looked reluctant, but he didn't have much choice. When Valerie set her mind to something, she did it.

Walking across the street to the looming building, Valerie neared the front door. The two men sitting on its steps eyed her suspiciously. She doubted she could go through the front door without raising some sort of alert about her presence, and so she kept walking around the side of the building.

She was looking for another way in. She was sure in a building so dilapidated, there must be a way.

Pulling at some of the boards covering the building's windows, most of them were securely fitted, but finally, one felt loose in her hands. She pulled it back to reveal a closed window.

Valerie looked around to make sure no one was watching. When she was satisfied she was alone, she pushed against the frame of the glass. The window popped up and slid, the old flaking brown paint turning into powder as it moved.

A stale air flowed out of the darkness inside. Valerie felt her heart racing, but there was no time for hesitation. She had an opportunity to get inside unseen, and she had to take it.

She pulled herself up and through the window, the board of wood settling back against the frame behind her, obscuring her entrance from any prying eyes.

Looking around, Valerie's eyes adapted to the dark. Just enough light from outside came through cracks in the boards covering the windows.

She saw that she was in an old bathroom. Once white tiles that had lined the walls were broken, lying on the floor, revealing the piping and wooden frames of the walls within.

To get a better look, Valerie took out her flashlight and scanned her environment. The beam lit up debris littered everywhere. Somewhere unseen, water was dripping.

*I better stay quiet*, she thought as she took tentative steps forward.

Avoiding stepping on the rubble of decay around her, she reached the door and pulled at its handle. The hinges groaned, but despite a little rusted resistance, the door opened.

Valerie found herself in a larger room. It looked like an old classroom of sorts. She wondered if the building had been a college back in the day.

No one was around, but Valerie was distinctly aware of a feeling. The feeling that things were moving around in other places nearby. She sensed she was not alone.

The shadows all around her cast doubt in her mind. She felt the danger of entering such a place. She could imagine how the killer, had he spent time in places like that, would have become accustomed to moving in the shadows.

He might even have become adept at it.

*Down*, Valerie thought. *I need to go underground.*

Moving through another doorway, she entered a long corridor. As she moved along it towards a stairwell at the end, she noticed what she thought was a bag of rags sitting in a doorway as she passed.

Suddenly, a hand emerged from the rags, and reached out.

Valerie gasped.

It was a man. He revealed his face, covered in grime and dirt.

"You wanna drink, honey?" the man said, pulling out what looked like a bottle of white spirit. Valerie could smell it on him.

"No... Thank you," Valerie said, trying her best not to appear unnerved.

Looking at the bottle in the man's hand, Valerie noticed that it carried a whiskey label. And yet the spirit inside was clear, like vodka or gin. The smell also reminded Valerie of old moonshine she'd discovered on a previous case.

"Where can a girl get some of her own around here?" Valerie asked.

The man grinned. "A woman after my own heart. Go downstairs. There's a panel in the basement next to the old boiler. Ask for Tom."

"Thank you," Valerie said, moving off towards the stairwell.

The man went back to his bottle.

Valerie was unnerved by the name he'd given her.

*Tom*, she thought. Flashes of the ring her own Tom had put on her finger back home came. She still didn't know what to do about that. Sometimes she was glad to have a case to take her away.

But not down there. Not in the darkness. Anywhere but the darkness.

Valerie reached the stairwell and descended. Down, down, down, floor after floor. She passed a handful of homeless people sleeping in doorways. Some acknowledged her, others slept or didn't move.

As she reached the basement, she began to feel like Alice going down the rabbit hole. Around her, there was evidence of people living, meeting, existing in the basement.

But she felt that it was only the tip of the iceberg.

Valerie looked around and saw a huge metal boiler that at one time would have heated the entire building. The grill in front of it looked like rusted teeth, and she half expected it to burst into life, flames spouting out of its mouth at her.

Next to it, just as the man in the doorway had said, was a gray panel. Valerie felt it with her hands. It was rough and scarred, but it moved. She slid her fingers down into a small ridge and pulled.

The panel popped open and, to Valerie's surprise, it opened like a door. Someone had even gone to the trouble of putting hinges on it.

Inside, she saw a huge, gaping hole in the wall, leading into an old tunnel. It looked like a piece of abandoned underground infrastructure. A disused sewer perhaps, or…

*An old subway maintenance tunnel*, she thought.

Her mind cast back to the first victim. The hatch in the subway, how the killer had gotten in and out without being seen. She imagined him moving around beneath the streets of Boston, able to emerge wherever he chose.

But what she didn't know was *why*. Why did he do it? What had caused such depraved and murderous behavior?

Picking up a piece of loose stone lying on the floor, Valerie wedged the panel open and stepped into the tunnel.

She moved along it, unsure of what she was now looking for or what she might find.

A smell meandered along the tunnel as she turned a corner. It was the unmistakable smell of white spirit. Though the tunnel moved off further into the shadows, Valerie found the source of the smell.

In a hole to the side was a room. And in that room, she could see several metal pots and some glass jars. Inside, clear white spirit could be seen.

"Moonshine," she whispered, her voice echoing.

"The best in the city," a man said, emerging from behind some of the equipment.

He looked remarkably presentable. In fact, given his pristine haircut, slicked back and shaved at the sides, and the expensive leather apron he had on, she was certain that the man wasn't homeless.

"You don't look like you belong here," Valerie said.

"And neither do you," the man answered immediately. "And yet, here we both are."

"You wouldn't be Tom, would you?" Valerie asked.

"That depends on who's asking," he replied. "And if she's with the law."

Valerie hadn't drawn her gun yet. She didn't want to throw fuel on the situation.

"Do you know a man has been murdered up above near here?" she asked.

"I hear things like that all of the time," he said, moving around the equipment and tinkering with a small tap where the spirit was dripping into a large clear bottle.

"And what else do you hear?" Valerie asked, nervous.

"You'd have to be more specific." He gazed back at Valerie through the large glass bottle. It skewed and distorted his face like a warped mirror.

"What about people using these tunnels to move around the city?"

He grinned, the glass warping his grin into a grotesque smile. "Sure, some do. But most come down here when they want something and then head back up to the streets once they've got it."

"Going by the number of inebriated people in the stairwell," Valerie prodded. "I assume you give them this moonshine in return for money."

"Oh, I don't know about that," the man said. "I like to think we provide a service."

"I'm not interested in your *business*," Valerie said. "But I am interested if you've run across anyone who might have bad-mouthed the drop-in center near here. Maybe they even had a problem with the staff?"

"Ah," he said. "So it was one of the volunteers that got killed. Ha!"

Valerie felt anger rising through her body. The man didn't care.

"What's so funny about someone being killed?"

"Well," he said, moving out from behind the glass bottle, "every day I get someone down here complaining about that place. About how they wouldn't give them food or help."

"Probably because they got abusive," Valerie explained.

"Probably," the man agreed. "Then they come here."

"And you give them what they need?"

"Sometimes," the man answered. "Other times I send them on their way."

"Tell me, then," Valerie said, never taking her eyes off the man for a moment. "Do you know of anyone who might have killed out of a grudge? Someone handy with a knife?"

Valerie noticed something. A flicker on the man's face. The mention of the knife had registered with him.

"Look," he said, moving around behind another large glass container, his shape warping with it. "I don't exactly want people down here who are going to have the law after them. That's bad for business."

"Then help me out," Valerie said. "If you think someone down here might be responsible, my quarrel is with them, not you."

The man turned and looked through the glass container. His eyes bulged, contorted by the clear liquid in front of them.

"Okay," he said. "There is someone. A man. He's good with a knife. And he spends a lot of time down here. But there's a small problem."

"And what's that?" Valerie asked, curious.

"He's standing behind you."

Valerie felt a cold chill run up her spine. She reached for her gun and turned. But something from the shadows was already upon her. A man with a pale face, strong and quick.

And his hands were wrapped around her neck.

He was too powerful. But Valerie had technique on her side. She pivoted her hips, grabbed the man by the collar, and threw him into the brick wall next to her.

A second pair of hands now reached out and grabbed her by the hair, yanking her backwards. She fell, smashing into the glass jars.

They cracked open, pouring out their innards all over the floor and Valerie.

Panic and horror ran through Valerie's mind.

She smelled the distilled spirit. She now couldn't use her gun. The slightest spark would not only ignite the liquid on the floor, but set her on fire.

Looking up she saw the man she had been talking to and his accomplice rushing towards her.

"The bitch has ruined the place!" one of them said.

"Careful," the other yelled. "The stove has a flame in it over there, the whole place will go up!"

Valerie looked along the floor and saw the spirit slowly creeping towards an upturned stove, naked flame and all. She only had moments to live.

Valerie staggered to her feet and threw a punch. The man dodged it and smashed Valerie across the jaw with his fist.

Searing pain ran up from her jaw. She was certain the man had broken one of her teeth. She felt a shard moving around in her mouth.

The man stood over her and pulled his fist back to strike again.

Valerie reach across floor and grabbed a broken piece of glass. She thrust it upward, catching the man between the ribs.

He let out a scream and fell back, landing on the floor and smacking his head against the concrete. Glancing along the floor, Valerie saw in abject terror that the liquid had nearly reached the upturned stove.

She and everything in that room was about to go up in the searing heat.

She had to escape.

Standing up, she rushed towards the tunnel outside the room, but the other attacker was still there. And now he was armed. A large knife glinted in the light of the flame. The man wielded it menacingly.

"We'll both die if we don't get out of here!" Valerie shouted.

"I ain't going back to prison," the man said, cold and detached.

Valerie knew a psychopath when she encountered one.

He slashed the knife sideways, catching Valerie's outstretched hand. She felt a sharp pain as it cut across her flesh. He then let out a kick, catching her in the stomach. She fell to the ground, dazed and in agony.

Looking up, she watched as the man readied himself for another attack.

He raised the knife again. But this time the hand stopped.

A piece of wood smashed across the back of his head and he crumpled to the ground.

Valerie looked up and saw Will holding the now broken plank of wood in disbelief at what he had just done. Charlie and Monaghan then appeared.

"Valerie!" Will shouted.

"The alcohol!" Valerie managed to get out. "It's going to blow!"

The three men rushed towards Valerie. Charlie lifted her up, pulling her out into the tunnel.

The spirit reached the flame.

And the tunnel shook with a deafening explosion.

# CHAPTER TWENTY TWO

Charlie hated hospitals. He hated the smell of them. The sterile walls. The feeling that wherever he was, he was always just a few rooms away from someone dying.

Another tragedy. Another loss.

He'd seen too many of them during his tours of duty. And yet, with the FBI, here he was in another one. This time, Boston General.

He waited patiently in the corridor outside of Valerie's room with Will. The doctor was tending to her, and they were waiting to see how she was doing.

It was a nervous wait.

"They've been in there quite a while," Will said.

Charlie knew now when Will was nervous. He did this thing where he tapped his knees with his fingers every now and then while sitting.

"It'll be okay," Charlie said. That was his hope at least.

Valerie had been through a lot. She was as tough as they came, but Charlie worried for her after the episode in the hotel with the night terror.

She wasn't right, not the way she used to be. He had felt it throughout the case. Something had been slowly eroding her stability even before they came to Boston. And now she'd just been in an explosion deep beneath city streets.

He feared her injuries would be enough to send her over the edge and that she would finally break.

The voices from the room were muffled, and even with Charlie's excellent hearing, he couldn't make out what was being said.

What he did hear was his phone suddenly coming to life.

The ring tone was unmistakable. It was his wife calling. This put him immediately on edge. Not because he didn't want to speak with his wife, but because he knew that his brother was still staying at their house. And where his brother went, trouble quickly followed.

"Hi, Baby," Charlie said, answering. "Everything okay?"

"Charlie, I'm scared."

Those words from Angela made Charlie stand up. He was in another city, hours away from his home. The idea that his wife was frightened and he wasn't there to make it better, made him sick.

"Talk to me, Honey. What's wrong? Are the kids okay?" he said as calmly as he could.

Will looked up at him from his chair in the corridor. He looked concerned at Charlie's change of tone.

The line buzzed slightly. " The kids are fine. Yesterday, I started noticing a car driving down our street. It slowed down while I was out getting the mail. I thought it was strange the way the driver sped up once he passed me."

"Did you see the driver?" Charlie asked, knowing that there must have been more to it. Angela wouldn't have been frightened by a car slowing down. She wasn't the jumpy, paranoid kind. She was as strong minded as they came. One of the many reasons Charlie loved her.

"The windows were tinted," Angela said. "But I got a real bad feeling about it. I tried to ignore it. But then a couple of hours later, I heard the same engine sound and so I looked out the window."

"The same car..." It wasn't a question, more a statement.

"Yeah," she answered. "And it slowed down again as it passed our house. I asked Marvin about it, but he said it was probably just someone lost."

"Did you see it again?" asked Charlie.

"Well that's the thing," Angela said. "Now I've seen it pass our house three separate times today. That's five in total. And each time it's slowed down. It can't be a coincidence."

"I'll deal with this, Baby, don't worry... Is Marvin there?"

"Yes, hold on."

Charlie heard Angela pass the phone to his brother.

"Hey, Brother, how's Boston?" Marvin asked, sounding a little too happy about the conversation. It seemed forced.

"Fine. Who's after you?" Charlie said abruptly.

There was a pause.

Marvin then laughed. "Don't worry, the car is nothing to do with me."

"You give me your word?"

"Sure," said Marvin. "Could it be something to do with your work, Charlie?"

"I don't know. "

"Will do," said Marvin. "But don't worry, I'll keep everyone safe if anyone tries anything."

"That's what I'm afraid of," said Charlie. "Just... Put Angela back on."

"Hey, Charlie," said Angela, still sounding worried.

"Look, Honey, it's probably nothing to worry about," Charlie said, trying to sound as reassuring as possible. "But I'm going to ask a friend at the local precinct to get a patrol car to check in on the house every few hours, okay?"

"Oh... Okay... I wish you were here, though."

"So do I," Charlie said. "Are the kids behaving themselves?"

"They're having a blast with Uncle Marvin."

"I bet they are," Charlie said, feeling his hackles go up.

The door to Valerie's hospital room opened and the doctor attending to her stepped into the corridor. Charlie nodded to him.

"Baby, I have to go," Charlie said, not wanting to worry Angela by telling her about what had happened. "I'll make that call, and if you get worried, phone 911, and call me right away. I love you."

"I love you too."

The call ended, Will stood up, and Charlie turned to the doctor.

"How is she?" Charlie asked.

"She's suffered some minor burns to her forearms and back," the doctor said.

"Will she need a skin graft?" asked Will. Charlie could sense he was holding back his emotions.

"No," the doctor said. "It's not that bad. If she keeps the burns dressed, she should heal within a couple of weeks. She also has a cut to her hand which we stitched up. And she has some particularly bad bruising on her spine."

The doctor stopped, and Charlie just felt relieved that Valerie's injuries weren't more serious.

"Gentlemen," the doctor then said. "Agent Law is asking to go straight back on duty. But I would advise she gets at least 24 hours rest to let the swelling around her back go down. We've done a scan and as far as I can see there's no permanent damage, but there's always a chance something will become more apparent over time. I think she needs some rest."

"Good luck telling her that," Will said.

"I am hoping you'll talk some sense into her," the doctor advised. "She really needs at least a day's rest, maybe more than that."

"Thank you doctor," said Charlie. "We'll do our best."

"If she decides to stay tonight, I'll check in on her later," the doctor said before walking down the corridor into his next patient's room.

"Thank God," Will said quietly. "I thought she was worse off than that when we brought her in."

"It's a miracle she didn't go up in flames during the explosion, Will," Charlie said. "I feel terrible for letting her go in there by herself."

"We're both guilty of that," answered Will. "But then, would we have been able to persuade her otherwise?"

Charlie knocked on the door and heard Valerie say, "come in."

They entered. Valerie was lying in a hospital bed. She had a number of cuts and scrapes over her face, and her cut hand had some bandages over it.

"Hey, Val," Charlie said, gently. "How you feeling?"

"Like I was in an explosion," she said, laughing then wincing in pain.

"Thank you for coming after me guys," she said. "But I reckon that was less than 30 minutes."

"We had a bad feeling," said Will. "We had to make sure you were okay."

"How's Monaghan?" asked Valerie.

"Despite the explosion, just as ruffled." Charlie sat down in a chair by Valerie's side.

"And the two perps in the tunnels?"

"They're alive and in custody. We've charged them with a list of crimes as long as your arm. But… You're not going to believe this," Charlie said. "Both of them have an alibi for the most recent murder. One was actually *inside* the  drop-in center trying to drum up business. And the other was seen across town at the time Gareth Kowalski was murdered."

"Damn…" Valerie sounded bitterly disappointed. "We went through all of that for nothing."

Charlie readied himself for a confrontation with his partner. "Val… The doctor…"

"I know what he's suggesting," she said, sounding annoyed. "But we don't have the manpower. I have to stay on the case until we catch this guy. He'll kill again. And soon. We have to stop him."

"Valerie," Will added. "Charlie and I are quite capable of carrying on the investigation while you recuperate."

"No," she said bluntly. "We don't have a suspect. We need to get back out into the streets and start canvassing the homeless population around that drop-in center again. It's our only hope."

Charlie didn't want to tell her the truth. It fluttered across his mind before he tucked it away again.

But it was too late. She had seen something.

Charlie and Valerie locked eyes. He could feel her examining his body language, his facial expressions, everything.

She looked shocked.

"Wait a minute..." she said. "Something has happened. What is it?"

Charlie and Will looked at each other.

"It's probably nothing," Will said.

As if in answer, a knock came at the door.

"Come in," Valerie said.

The door opened and in stepped one Detective Monaghan. He wore some of the same scrapes on his face as Valerie from the explosion, but he was still in one piece.

"How are you feeling, Valerie?" he asked.

"Valerie?" she smiled. "First time I've heard you call me that. I'm fine Detective Monaghan... Hank..."

He smiled back at her.

"Any developments?" she asked.

"Just the suspect we're looking into," he said, sounding as if he thought Valerie knew all about it. "Will and Charlie were just waiting for me to take them down to the crime scene and fill them in on the way."

She didn't know anything about that.

They had barely just been informed about it themselves, but Charlie and Will had kept it from her, and Charlie knew that would cause issues with Valerie.

Valerie glanced at them both in accusatory fashion. "Go on, Hank."

"Less than an hour ago a tourist couple from England took a wrong turn into a rough part of the city."

"Are they okay?" she asked.

"They are," he continued. "But they were attacked by a man wielding a knife. They said he looked homeless. One of the tourists was ex-army, so he put up a good fight, scared the guy off. He ran away and..."

"And what?" Valerie pushed herself up on her hands so she was sitting up completely in the bed. Her eyes were intense and fiery.

Charlie knew that meant trouble.

"The doctor is recommending Valerie rests," Charlie interjected.

"Don't listen to him, Hank. I'm fine. Go on."

Charlie felt frustrated. He didn't want her jeopardizing herself or the case if she was diminished by her injuries. He could tell she was in a lot of pain.

"The man ran off into what's known as a culvert," Hank said.

"What's a culvert?" asked Valerie.

"It's a tunnel that carries river water through it."

There was a silence in the room. It was almost palpable.

Valerie turned to Will and Charlie.

"It's probably nothing, you said!" she sounded mad. "A homeless man, attacks someone with a knife, and then runs into a tunnel under the ground? And that doesn't sound *exactly* like our perp?"

"We just want you to get better, Valerie," Will said.

"The only way I'm going to get better," she said, pulling the blanket back and stepping out of the bed, wincing in pain. "Is if we catch this guy once and for all."

# CHAPTER TWENTY THREE

"Quoth the raven, 'nevermore,'" Valerie said as she, Will, and Charlie walked down a street past a statue of Edgar Allan Poe, and towards the next crime scene. It lay between a row of suburban houses.

"Boston's most famous writer," Charlie remarked.

"I always was partial to Poe, you know," said Will. "His death is still an enduring mystery. He seems to have disappeared for a few hours on the day of his death only to reappear wearing someone else's clothes and in a delirious state. He died a few hours later, and he was unable to tell anyone what had happened to him."

"I always thought he was a tragic figure," said Valerie. "But I think this city is intent on holding onto as many mysteries and unsolved crimes as it can. Let's hope ours isn't one of them."

Valerie felt the burns under their dressings. Her forearms had taken the brunt of the fire, but she had been lucky. The gel the hospital had on the dressings kept them cool for now, and the painkillers coursed through her body, numbing the pain a little.

Looking ahead, Valerie saw the forlorn figure of Detective Monaghan standing on the roadside. The area was no longer cordoned off, but a few police officers were still present.

"This is where the attack happened," Monaghan said as he approached, not wasting time with any formalities.

"And the two victims got away?" Valerie asked.

Monaghan nodded. "One of them managed to fight their attacker off. They struggled over a knife, and the killer clearly felt it wasn't worth the risk any more. He ran off down this lane." He pointed to the side.

Valerie looked down a small lane that cut between two suburban houses. At the end of it, she could see a railing and what looked to be very old brickwork.

Monaghan scratched his unshaven chin. "The culvert... The tunnel that carries a tributary from the Boston river under the east side of the city can be found down there. The attacker ran down through it when he escaped."

"Do we know if that's where he emerged from in the first place?" Charlie asked.

"No," answered Monaghan. "But he seemed to make a beeline for it. That means…"

"He knew the entrance to the tunnel was there," Will concluded.

Valerie looked around. The street they were standing on was a suburban one. Houses lined each side. She puzzled over it. It was different from the other places where the killer had struck. There was no obvious homeless population there.

"Are the witnesses on site?" Valerie asked.

"Yes," Monaghan answered. "Follow me."

They walked quietly to the back of a parked police car. Monaghan opened the back door revealing two frightened looking people in their forties.

"This is Margaret and James Bradley," Monaghan said.

The couple stepped out of the car. Valerie instantly noticed their clothes. The man was wearing an I Love Boston t-shirt and the woman had a handbag with a Union Jack on it, proudly displaying where she came from.

"This is Agent Law from the FBI and her colleagues," Monaghan told them.

"Mr. and Mrs. Bradley," Valerie said. "Quite a scare you had today, but you may just have fought off a dangerous serial killer. Well done."

"My word," Margaret replied in a strong English accent. "I could tell he was evil the second we saw him. Couldn't I, James?"

"Yes, Dear," the man said, sounding as though he had said those exact words a million times over in response to something his wife had said.

"Mr. Bradley," Charlie stuck out his hand and shook the man's. "I'm ex-army. I hear you served in Iraq with the British Army. Always nice to meet a brother from the service."

"And you," James said. His eyes lit up and he relaxed at Charlie's words.

"I guess you used your hand-to-hand training on your attacker?" Charlie asked. "Can you tell us what happened, exactly?"

"Well, me and the Mrs., we was headin' to take a photo of that Edgar Allan Poe statue. We was walking back down here and we stopped at the corner. We was lost, wasn't we Maggie?"

"Yes, we were," Margaret replied enthusiastically.

"Then what happened?" asked Will.

"Well, I sees this fella," James said. "He's looking about with this smile on his face. Ye know? Like somebody goin' down memory lane. So I stop and ask him if he knows the way to the nearest subway."

"And how did he react to that?" asked Valerie. She was keenly interested in what the man's behavior was at the point of contact. A feeling, if not a theory about the killer, was finally bubbling away at the back of her mind.

"He looks at me like I've just tried to get me leg over on his old mam," James answered. "Before I knew what was what, he's got a knife in his hand. Practically frothin' at the mouth like a mad dog."

"Now, I'm no spring chicken. I've seen a bit. And I got my hands to fall back on if I'm ever in a pinch. So I block the knife and send a palm strike to the nose. Pow!" James imitated the strike with lightning and gregarious effect.

"And he ran off after that?" asked Will.

"Indeed he did," he said. "I watched him climb over that railin' down there. I chased after him, and then I saw him disappear in that tunnel under the lane. I like to think I'm brave an' all, but I weren't about to go down there into the dark. Not without a weapon."

"Quite right," said Charlie. "You did more than enough. Is there anything else that struck you about the man?"

"Only the smell," James said.

"Bad was it?" Charlie asked.

"No, no," he answered. "He smelled of very strong aftershave, a bit like the stuff I remember my dad wearing back in the day. I was surprised because he looked homeless."

"If you wouldn't mind," Valerie said. "Would you be able to describe what his face looked like?"

"Maggie here's got a better memory than me," James said, laughing.

"It's true!" she said. "He forgot where his glasses were the other night, and they were on his head!"

The two laughed together, and Valerie thought that they were the type of down to earth people she'd have had a good time sharing a few drinks with.

But now was not the time for that. They were close to the killer. She could feel it.

"If I get an artist, could you work with him on a sketch of the man?" Valerie asked.

"I'm no good at drawin'," she said.

"She means the artist'll do the drawin' Luv," James joked. And then they were both laughing again.

"Yes, no problem," Margaret finally said.

"Thank you," Valerie shook their hands and walked back towards the lane where the tunnel entrance was.

She stood out on the street, looking down the lane and then around.

"What's wrong?" asked Monaghan as the others approached.

"This attack doesn't fit the pattern," Valerie said.

"What do you mean?" Monaghan seemed intrigued.

"All of the other attacks took place where there was an evident homeless population," Valerie said.

"That's true," Will agreed.

"Yeah, I haven't seen any sign of that here in this part of the city," Charlie added.

"But what could that mean?" Monaghan prodded.

Valerie thought it through for a moment.

"Everything so far has been connected with the homeless scene," she finally said. "Except this. So, maybe the killer wants us to think that's what's important here."

"A ruse?" asked Charlie.

"Think about what James Bradley just told us," said Valerie. "The man smelled of strong aftershave. How many homeless people care about that sort of a thing? Or have access to aftershave?"

"I suppose he could have got it from a drop-in center or as a donation somewhere," Charlie mused.

"Maybe," said Valerie, unconvinced. "Or maybe he's not what he seems. He's dressing up as a homeless person for some reason."

"It doesn't seem to me," said Will, "that he's trying to lead us down a path. He's probably not even aware of the investigation into him."

"That's true," said Valerie. "Then we need to start thinking more about the profile. What does a man dressed up as a homeless person and wearing strong aftershave say about him?"

"That he can't commit to the role," Charlie said. "He hates the smell of the streets."

"Exactly, Charlie," Valerie said.

"Maybe he used to be homeless," Monaghan finally interjected, his voice as gruff as ever. "Maybe he hates them because he was one of them. Like a self-hate. A lot of violent offenders pick on what they really hate about themselves, and then beat on people who represent that."

Valerie was surprised, but she chastised herself internally that she shouldn't have been. Detective Monaghan was a seasoned professional, and he knew the great city of Boston and its quirks more than anyone.

"Excellent stuff, Detective," Will said, echoing Valerie's thoughts.

"I think we're onto something here," she said. "So he's not homeless, but he dresses like he is. Maybe he does hate what they represent, but then why come here to a suburb? There must be something…"

Valerie's thoughts trailed off. In a sea of possibilities, a theory was forming. She looked at the houses around her. And then to the lane. Over the back of it was a high wall, and beyond it, a house that looked older and larger than the others.

She rushed down the lane towards it.

"Valerie?" Will said.

But she wasn't listening. She was thinking. She was formulating. Reaching the wall, she stretched up and pulled herself up onto it.

Looking over, there was a courtyard behind it, and a sandstone house beyond that.

Charlie and the others caught up.

"Climbing walls, Valerie?" he said. "What's over there?"

"A landmark," she said. "A point of interest just next to this culvert."

Pulling out her phone, she looked at the area on her map app. Pinching in to zoom on the screen, the phone automatically honed in on their location.

And then she saw it. The house on its own.

"That place is a temporary foster shelter," she said, hopping down from the wall.

"Oh my," mused Will. "You don't think he was here because of it?"

"I do!" Valerie said, excitedly. "The killer is telling us a story."

"A story?" said Monaghan.

"Think about it," she continued, her voice deadened by the walls of the lane. "The subway. The alleyway. The  drop-in center. Now this foster shelter. He's telling us his narrative without realizing it. He's visiting locations from *his* past. I'm certain of it."

"When you mentioned that he *used* to be homeless. That made it click. All of this is to do with who he used to be."

"An interesting theory," said Will. "Would it be possible to identify him based on these locations?"

"I'm not sure," answered Monaghan. "But if he *was* in that foster home at some point, we might be able to narrow it down to suspects of his age."

"Especially if they have a record of violent behavior," said Charlie. "And something in their personal history that links to his proficiency with a knife."

"Monaghan," said Valerie. "Could you search the foster care records and see if anyone was placed there…"

"What time frame?" asked Monaghan.

"Well, we think the suspect could sit outside of the normal age range for a serial killer," said Will. "He could be in his early twenties, he could be fifty. I would say anything from 45 years ago until about 15 years ago would safely cover it. If the killer was in that foster home, it would have been at some point across that time frame."

"Fantastic," Monaghan said, clapping his hands together enthusiastically.

Valerie was surprised. She'd never seen him animated. But she understood. It was a lead. And it was about time they had one.

"I'll call as soon as I find anything," he said, rushing back along the lane and disappearing from view.

"If only we knew the significance of these locations," Will said. "We might be able to predict where he'd go next."

"I know," Valerie said in a somber tone.

Then she heard a sound that almost froze her heart. A woman's cackling laugh came from further down the lane.

"Are you OK Val?" Charlie asked, clearly seeing the change in her demeanor

"I… I'm fine."

The laugh came again. This time louder than before. Valerie could tell she was the only one who heard it.

*It's only in your mind, it's only in your mind,* she started thinking over and over.

But she couldn't help herself. She still had to look. She moved off towards the railing at the back of the lane where the killer had disappeared down a tunnel.

She could feel Charlie and Will looking at each other, worried.

The laugh came again. And with it, Valerie quickened her pace.

She looked over the railing, expecting to see the image of her sickly mother in a straightjacket, laughing at her. But all she saw was a trickling of water, passing down below and into a dark, brick tunnel beneath the streets.

Will stepped alongside Valerie. "What do you see?"

At first, Valerie thought she'd have to spin a lie as to why she was looking down there to hide the hallucination But luck was shining on her in that moment.

Her keen observational skills had caught something.

"Is that blood on the brickwork?" she asked.

"Where?" Charlie looked, peering over the railing.

"There," Valerie said. "Third brick down. Hold on."

Before Will or Charlie could stop her, Valerie pulled herself up over the railing and carefully climbed down to the mouth of the tunnel.

"I'm right," she said. "It's blood! And it looks like there's a trail down here."

Valerie took out her flashlight. They were in luck, the water was at an extremely low level. She moved the beam around, following droplets of blood along the inside of the tunnel wall.

"He must have cut his hand and is bleeding from it," she said. "It looks quite fresh."

Charlie appeared behind her. "We could follow that."

"Uh, a little help please, guys?" Will said, half dangling from the railing.

Charlie put his hand up and helped Will down. His feet splashed into the inch thin, murky water that smelled like stale garbage.

"A trail of breadcrumbs?" Will said, approaching the tunnel.

"I'm going after it," Valerie said. She felt she had something to prove. The cackled laughter she had just heard wasn't the first time she had imagined her mother nearby.

She had to prove to herself that she was still strong enough to enter dangerous places and keep her head.

"I'll come with you," said Charlie.

"No dice, Charlie. Look." Valerie moved her flashlight beam further along the tunnel. A large metal grate covered the hole to stop it from getting blocked with debris during a flood.

Valerie moved up to the grating. She eyeballed the gap between the bars.

"I'll fit through here, but you won't, Charlie."

Charlie grabbed the metal bars and pulled. They were stuck in place. He sighed. Valerie could tell he knew she was right.

"If I'm not back…"

"Wait a minute, Val," Charlie said. "We just got you out of the hospital. You're not going underground by yourself again. Please."

"I'll fit through there," Will said, trying his best not to get his feet wet.

"Will, I don't think…"

"Val," said Charlie. "You can write me up for insubordination. You can have my badge. But we nearly lost you today. And the doctor said you weren't recovered. I won't let you go down there alone. It's either Will or I'm picking you up and carrying you out of here."

Valerie didn't know whether to be angry or moved.

"You could try," she said. "But I don't go quietly."

"I know," said Charlie. "Will it is, then." Charlie opened up his jacket, took out his revolver and handed it to Will. "Just like I've been showing you at the gun range."

Will looked nervous. But he nodded, took the gun, then made sure the safety was still on.

Valerie admired his bravery, though as much as she valued his psychological advice, she would have preferred going after a dangerous killer with Charlie by her side.

He was a dangerous man if he was your enemy.

"We'll see how far the blood trail goes," she said. "If we're not…"

"I'll try and find another entrance into this tunnel system," Charlie said. "I'll contact city hall and see if they can help with some old plans. Be careful. Both of you."

Valerie pushed between the grating until she was through. With a little more effort, Will tried.

"I think I'm stuck."

"You're not stuck," Charlie said. "You've just been behind a desk too long." He pushed Will until he too was on the other side.

Valerie waved to Charlie and then moved off, following the blood trail, wondering if the killer was waiting just around the next bend, knife in hand and hell bent on murder.

# CHAPTER TWENTY FOUR

Valerie felt the coldness of the tunnels. The brickwork seemed to be soaking up any ambient heat and turning it to cold. If she didn't know any better, she would have said the place emitted an icy chill.

She and Will had been walking for several minutes. The dried blood trail continued, albeit sometimes intermittently.

But the drops were still there, smears of it against the walls occasionally, too. Valerie was certain he had a bad cut on his hand.

She could hear Will's nervous breathing alongside her. She felt for him. This was not the type of environment that he was used to; but then, it wasn't a place Valerie was used to either, walking around beneath the world in the darkest of places.

"You okay?" Valerie asked in a hushed tone.

"Yes," Will said quietly. "I wonder how far these tunnels go?"

"Charlie will hopefully find out where it comes out and meet us there," Valerie said, hopefully. "Unless we find the killer down here."

"Or he finds us first," Will said, still whispering. "I just hope we catch the bastard."

"We will," she said. "But I'm not sure he's near. This blood trail is at least a couple of hours old."

Valerie felt Will's determination. He had always wanted to help the world by catching such killers, but this one seemed more personal to him. It had from the very first moment they visited that alleyway.

"Will," Valerie asked. "You don't need to tell me. And I know this is a strange place to ask. But what is it about this case? It's affected you in a way I've never seen. And I feel it's to do with the homeless people we've encountered."

Will sighed. "I don't want you thinking I'm bringing baggage to this case."

"We all have baggage," Valerie said.

Something echoed further along the tunnel. Valerie felt the hairs go up on the back of her neck. She beamed her flashlight down to the end of it. But all she saw was another bending tunnel, moving again to some unanticipated part of the city.

"Perhaps this isn't the best place," Will said.

"The blood we're following is dry," Valerie said. "He passed here a while ago, and the sound won't reach him as it'll be absorbed by these walls and the bends in the tunnels. And if I'm honest, it would be nice to talk. This place plays tricks with your ears." She thought back to the sound of her mother's cackled laugh. She was terrified of hearing it down there. It was smartest to stay quiet, but Valerie knew the silence could bring with it a hallucination And that could break her down there.

"Okay," Will replied, moving forward in the dark. "During my Ph.D. study about twenty years ago, I was assigned several post graduate students to work with. You know how it is, you help them with their studies, they help you with some of the grunt work on your research programs."

"Where was this?"

"A college in Massachusetts," he said, continuing. "One of my fellow Ph.D. students was named Katrina. She was everything a person could be at their best. Kind. Insightful. Intelligent. Talented."

"Beautiful?" Valerie asked.

The sound in Will's voice made her think Katrina was extra special to him.

"I know I shouldn't have," he said. "But we became romantically involved. It was a breach of my ethics to get involved with a colleague. But we were close in age, and she was so mesmerizing to me. I fell for her."

"And what happened to her?"

"About seven months into her postgraduate work, she started growing distant. She was late submitting papers. I tried to cover for her. Her work became sloppy. And she was increasingly irritable with everyone, including me. But no matter how much I asked, she wouldn't tell me what was wrong.

"It was around that time I first noticed the needle marks on her arms." Will stopped for a moment and rubbed his brow.

Everything about his voice and posture told a story. And it wasn't one that ended well.

"Are you okay?" Valerie asked.

"Yes," he said, walking on. "I just haven't mentioned this to... Well, anyone really."

Valerie felt a sense of pride that he would confide in her. But then, they had been through much together.

"I asked her about the needle marks, but she swore it was for a medication she had to take. I naively believed her... One day," he said.

"I found a note. She had quit the college. She said she couldn't stay in a relationship with me, either. And that she was heading home to stay with her family.

"I wanted to respect her decision, as much as it broke my heart. I'd never felt about a woman like that before. Not to such depths." Will's voice swirled down the tunnel with the trickle of water at their feet.

He continued: "But as the days past, I felt compelled to reach out to her. To confess my undying love, so to speak. That I couldn't live without her. After a some digging, I found her mother, but she hadn't spoken to Katrina in years. It had all been a lie."

"By all accounts, Katrina's father had been abusive, and so she had moved out the moment she was old enough to. She didn't just blame her father, she also blamed her mother for never leaving him, opening her up to the abuse."

"I assured Katrina's mother I would track her down for both of us. I won't bore you with the details of how I found her, but after many weeks of searching, I was reliably informed she had been homeless for months as her addiction worsened. I tracked down her dealer and he said she was sleeping in an old, abandoned factory floor."

"And was she?" Valerie asked.

"I knew as soon as I entered that old building," he said. His voice cracked as if on the verge of tears. "It was the smell you see. You never forget it."

"Oh, no…" Valerie knew instantly what he meant.

"I… I found her body. Or what the rats had left of it."

"I'm so sorry, Will." She stopped and felt compelled to give him a hug.

"It's okay," he said, wiping the tears from his eyes. "It was a long time ago. I think seeing all those people who had fallen through the same safety nets as Katrina had… It just brought it back. Well… Now you know why I've been struggling with this."

"When we get out of here, we can have a proper talk about it, Will," Valerie said, smiling at him in the dark, their faces lit only by the reflections of the flashlight on the water and brickwork.

They moved ahead, their footsteps sloshing through the trickling water. Nothing more was said between them for several minutes as they continued to follow the drops of blood.

Will suddenly stopped.

"Can you hear that?"

Valerie strained her ears. It reminded her of the noise she'd first heard as a child when putting a sea shell to her ear. A swishing, swirling sound.

Will turned his attention to something above them. His face bore a grim expression.

"What is it?" Valerie asked, nervously.

He touched a brown line on the brickwork above them. It glistened with damp.

"I think when there's a water surge from the Charles river, this tributary fills up. And I think that's what that sound is."

"What do we do?" Valerie asked, suddenly realizing she sounded like a lost child down there turning to a father.

"We can't go back, the water is flowing towards us from that direction. If the surge is coming, it's coming with it." He continued to listen.

The sound of rushing water was closer, growing in volume every second.

Valerie turned her flashlight to the rear and looked back along the long thin tunnel.

Her blood ran cold.

The light caught something moving back there. It contorted and writhed like a sea of undulating serpents heading straight for them.

The water foamed and cascaded up the walls. In moments, it would be on them, and there would be no escape. No daylight. No air.

Valerie now felt the horror that her need to prove herself could lead to such a horrible death.

"Run!" Will said, grabbing Valerie by the hand.

They rushed along the tunnel as fast as they could. Soon, Valerie overtook Will, and it was she who led him.

He fell, tripping over something.

Valerie picked him up, eyeing the oncoming rush of water behind them. It roared like a monstrous creature desperate to consume them.

"Come on!" Valerie screamed.

They were moving again. But not fast enough. The water was relentless in its desires.

They moved around a bend, and then down another section of tunnel. Then another turn. One blind corner after another, heading deeper, deeper still into the darkness, into the cold subterranean world beneath Boston.

Will was flagging behind. Gasping as he ran out of steam.

"Leave me…" he said. "Keep going…"

"No!" Valerie yelled. "We're getting out of here."

They were at a cross section. Valerie didn't know where to go; she flashed the beam of her flashlight around. It caught a spot of red on the wall.

This time it glistened wet.

Valerie grabbed Will's arm and practically dragged him that direction. She was counting on the killer knowing the safe way out, and they would use that to their advantage.

The roar of the water behind was now deafening. Will said something, but Valerie couldn't make it out.

She felt something cold, the water pushing an icy blast of air through the tunnel behind them.

Desperately she ran. Desperately she dragged Will on his feet behind her.

The water, just a few inches behind was ready to consume them.

*A light!* she screamed in her mind. She could see it up ahead. Light coming in from somewhere.

She rushed in the direction. She padded the ground with her feet; her arms ached with the burns and the weight of pulling her friend behind her.

They ran together. They gasped for air.

An icy swoosh sounded as Valerie's ears were covered in water. The river hit her, striking her body like a train. She was thrown around the inside of the tunnel against the brickwork.

But she never let go of her friend.

The water surged them through the tunnel towards the light. It grew brighter. Valerie held her breath, no matter how much she desperately wanted to inhale.

That would mean certain death.

The water pushed them both, a tangled mess, into the light. Valerie felt them fall for a moment. She reached out, seeing something at the last moment. A large rusting pipe.

She grabbed hold with one hand. The other holding onto her friend.

Looking down, she was hanging over a large swirling drain. The water was pouring into it like a waterfall, and she was still in the water's path. She gasped for air when she could.

Will dangled from her arm. He flailed trying to grab for another piece of the large pipe which jutted out from the brickwork.

But he couldn't reach.

Valerie screamed, feeling the weight of her friend pulling her down. It was as if something was separating in her shoulder. The ligaments, the tendons giving in. Her will wanting what her body could not provide.

Valerie looked down and caught Will's gaze.

Her hand was slipping on the pipe. Soon they would both fall into the pool of water below.

Will gave her a look. His eyes filled with affection.

"Let go," he said.

"No!"

"Valerie," he said gently, his voice barely audible beneath the roar. "It's okay."

"No, Will!"

Will pulled at her hand, releasing her grip from his arm.

Valerie screamed as she watched him fall into the water far below. The water pulled him down into a dark tunnel, and he was gone.

Tears streamed down Valerie's face. She wanted to let go and find him. But she knew it was impossible. The water had taken him, and it would take her, too.

She thought of Tom. She thought of his smiling face as she said yes to his marriage proposal. She thought of them listening to old records together. She thought of him kissing her good night.

Reaching up, she grabbed the piping with both hands. And with what strength she had left, she pulled herself up and onto a metal walkway.

She lay there for a minute sobbing.

Wearily, she pulled herself up onto her feet.

The large, cavernous room had a couple of maintenance walkways moving around.

But that was not what caught her eye.

She realized someone was looking at her. From behind a veil of falling water, the blurred outline of a man stood across the room on another walkway.

She couldn't see his features. But the eyes. She could feel them boring into her. It was the killer. He turned and disappeared into a tunnel behind him, the darkness swallowing him up.

Crying, Valerie smashed her clenched fist into the metal railing in front of her.

"I will find you!" she screamed. "You'll pay for this!"

She looked down to the water below, the grave that took her friend. Valerie would avenge Will. She started to climb the railing, dripping wet, but relentlessly fueled by an anger she had never felt before.

She would chase the killer now to the ends of the Earth.

# CHAPTER TWENTY FIVE

Charlie waited impatiently in the cold gray corridor of Boston Hall for the civil engineer.

He had tried to reach Valerie and Will several times by phone, but each time there had been no possibility of connection. They were deep under the city streets, and their phones simply couldn't work covered over by concrete, bricks, and earth.

"Come on," he said to himself, pacing up and down in the corridor.

A fear he had rarely felt in his life was washing over him. It was a dread he had experienced during his tours of duty. The feeling that your team was out there somewhere. In danger or worse.

Charlie turned to the office door nearest him and raised his fist to bang on it.

But the door abruptly opened.

Out stepped a woman in thick black glasses.

"I'm terribly sorry it took so long, Agent Carlson," she said. "I had a damned time trying to find the old blueprints. You know, those tunnels were laid well over a hundred years ago to help with flood water from the Charles River. It's actually a fascinating story, you see..."

"I'm sorry, Miss Danvers, I don't have time," he said. "My partners are running around down in those tunnels and they've been gone too long. I have to know where they come out!"

"Of course," she said. "Come in here."

They stepped into the office. There were stacks of files and old papers. Miss Danvers did not keep an organized office. But then, that didn't could for much. Some of the most brilliant people Charlie knew were disorganized.

Miss Danvers moved over to her desk and pushed some papers off onto the floor. She then rolled out an old blueprint onto the surface.

"Now, let me see," she said.

To Charlie, the sketches were just a collection of lines and measurements, but Miss Danvers clearly saw those lines in their real world context.

She ran her finger along one of the lines. "I believe this is the tributary from the river. If we follow it, here it comes to the open section behind the houses you mentioned, not far from Poe's statue."

"Great, but where does it come out?" he said, sweat beading on his forehead.

Miss Danvers pointed to a section. "The only exit I can see that's within a mile of that piece of tunnel is an old service passage that enters Balenthaul Train Station. Other than that, you'd be walking for miles before you found another way out. That is, if the surges didn't get you."

"Surges?" Charlie asked, concerned.

"Water surges from the river," Miss Danvers explained. "They quite often fill up those tunnels at a moment's notice. They'd be deadly if you were down there when it happened."

"My God..." said Charlie. "Thank you." He ran out of the building at speed, fumbling for his phone.

Dialing quickly, he didn't waste any time as he jumped into his car. "Monaghan!" he shouted over the phone. "Get some officers to Balenthaul train station. There's a way into the tunnels there. We've got to find them before they drown."

"Jesus," Monaghan said, gruffly. "Okay. I'll meet you there. I have something for you as well."

The call ended.

Charlie turned the ignition and sped off.

He negotiated traffic as quickly as he could, moving around corners with force and weaving in and out of slower vehicles.

His phone rang and he put it on speaker.

"Monaghan?"

"Charlie?"

He knew the sound of Angela's voice immediately. "Honey, this isn't..."

"Charlie, someone was in our backyard last night," she said, her voice wavering. "Christ, they looked into our kids' bedroom window!"

Charlie's heart raced. He didn't know what to do. He was hours from his family. And he had a growing dread that the people showing an unhealthy interest in his home were looking for his brother, Marvin.

Passing cars were one thing, but someone on their property was another.

"Charlie, I'm scared. Really scared. Please come home."

Charlie took a sharp corner and the car nearly spun out of control, but he grabbed the wheel and tamed the drift.

Angela obviously heard the noise. "Charlie, are you okay?"

"Yeah, Honey," he said. "I'll be on the next flight out. Valerie and Will are missing."

"Oh no…" Angela sighed on the phone.

"But you and the kids come first," he said, grimly. Thinking of his friends stuck in the cold dark of those tunnels with water surging over them. "I'll be home in a few hours, Honey. In the meantime, call the cops if you get concerned before I get there."

"Okay, Charlie. I love you."

"I love you, too. I'll deal with this, don't you worry."

The call ended, but as it did, Charlie's concentration broke. A car came out from an unmarked crossing and he only saw it at the last second. He swerved and felt a crushing jolt through his body as the car smashed into a street light.

# CHAPTER TWENTY SIX

Valerie saw the blood on the rungs of the ladder leading up from the darkness.

*He came this way,* she thought. Grabbing hold of the ladder, she pulled herself up one by one, her clothes heavy from the surge water.

Her hair was soaked, hanging down in front of her face, and her body ached. The burns on her arms were beginning to show their pain as the water had washed away the cooling gel the hospital had put on.

But something fueled her onward, even though her body did not want to continue.

It was grief. The loss of Will. And pure, unadulterated rage at the killer he had died chasing.

She pulled herself up into a room. Light streamed in through a doorway to another tunnel. Through it, she realized she was now in a rail tunnel.

Limping up ahead, she moved. One step at a time alongside the rail until her eyes were struck by sunshine outside.

She emerged and saw droplets of blood on the platform edge.

*He pulled himself up onto the platform, here,* she thought.

Valerie did the same, but she could feel the damage to her shoulder. The damage that had been done while trying to pull Will up to safety.

A flash of his face just before he fell filtered through her mind. She held back the tears.

Looking around, she touched her revolver in its holster. Still there. It had been immersed in water, but Valerie knew the bullets were waterproof, so it *should* still fire if needed, though it might not be reliable.

She didn't want to alarm any of the passengers standing on the platform by brandishing her gun. But she'd keep it close.

Valerie heard a sound. It was a swooshing noise coming from the tunnel she'd come from. At first she shivered, thinking it to be the surge water coming to claim her.

But it was the sound of a train nearing.

In the opposite direction another train was hurtling down the track towards the station. Two trains meeting there, crossing paths at the same time.

In Valerie's mind there was a fate to that. She was there to cross paths with a murderous killer. And she was hell bent on bringing his killing spree to a halt.

Valerie moved along the platform as the trains neared. The passengers moved to the platform edge. One girl she noticed playing music loudly on her phone with no headphones.

She stepped to the platform edge.

Valerie felt drawn to her for some reason. It was almost as if she knew the girl would play a part in the crossing of paths. There was a reason the killer might target *her* more than any other. A theory was building in her head, but it hadn't quite come to fruition yet.

The sound of the train in the tunnel reached a crescendo. And as it did so, Valerie watched in horror. Water dripped down her face from her hair. And the unmistakable shape of the man from the tunnel appeared

Valerie saw him running through a group of passengers. But not away. And not towards Valerie, either. He was running towards the girl at the edge of the platform.

Drawing her gun, Valerie screamed. "Everyone down, FBI!"

But there was too much confusion. People froze to the spot and the killer took advantage.

Valerie tried to get a clear shot, but there were innocent bystanders in the way.

The girl playing her music, barely a teenager, turned at the last moment as the killer wrapped his arms around her, picked her up in the air, and then threw her onto the tracks in front of one of the oncoming trains.

People screamed for help as the girl crashed to the ground on the tracks. Valerie ran as quickly as she could. With every ounce of energy left in her body, she rushed along the platform.

But she was too far away.

The train honked its horn desperately and its brakes screeched. But the hulking mass of metal could not stop in time.

The girl tried to get to her feet, dazed and in shock, just as the train reached her. Valerie let out a horrible cry of failure. Passengers turned away in utter terror so as not to see the girl crushed to death.

Then, Valerie saw something. A flash of something moving from the opposite platform. Something gray. Something bold. Something brave.

It moved in front of the girl and the two became one. The gray figure pulled the girl out of the way and up onto the platform.

The crowd erupted in relieved shouts of joy and celebration.

Squeezing through the circle of onlookers, Valerie finally saw the truth. The girl was alive and well. And she was lying in the arms of a very tired, and a very wet, Doctor Will Cooper.

And the killer had vanished yet again in the commotion.

*

Valerie sat on a platform bench, exhausted. Will sat beside her, equally out of it.

"I thought you were gone," she said, holding back tears.

"So did I," said Will. "The water carried me to the other side of the station. There's another hatch over there. I managed to grab on and get out before I drowned. Not quite sure how I did it, to be honest."

"Because you're stronger than you think," Valerie said. "And I'm very glad of that."

"The killer?" Will asked.

"Escaped," Valerie said forlornly. "To where, I don't know. Probably another location in his history. But without his background, how can we know?"

"I might be able to help with that," said a gruff voice standing over them.

"Monaghan…" Valerie smiled.

"You two look like you've been through it," he said.

"How is the girl?" asked Will.

"She's dazed, but nothing permanent," he said. "You did good, Will."

"Thank you," he said.

Monaghan held out a couple of pieces of paper in his hand. Crumpled as usual, as if he had stuffed them into his pocket.

"What's that?" asked Valerie.

"I ran those checks at the foster care home," Monaghan said.

"Was I right?" Valerie asked, hopefully.

"See for yourself," Monaghan grinned, handing the papers to her.

Valerie looked at them. Instantly, she saw the eyes on the page staring back at her. She knew it was the killer. She just *knew it*.

Scanning the man's history, she saw it all laid out before her. The connections were buzzing in her mind.

"Frederick Pitt, 47 years old," she turned to the exhausted Will next to her. "We were right, he's outside the usual range."

"What else do you see?" Will said, sounding weak.

"His family history is here," she said. "His mother was homeless and took him around the streets of Boston until he was twelve. The state tried to take him from her, and she hid around Boston. I bet she took him down into those tunnels."

"It's probable," Will said. "He certainly knows them well enough."

Valerie continued: "He was put into the care home we saw, but his mother busted him out and they disappeared. That was until she was found dead… In a harbor with a knife in her throat."

"That might explain his obsession with the knife," Will offered.

"Yeah," agreed Valerie. "I think this entire pattern is about his mom and what happened to her."

"They never found her killer," Monaghan said. "And Frederick ended up in several places over the years. His psych report says he refused to talk with therapists about what happened to his mother. Do you think he killed her?"

"No," said Valerie. "This isn't about hatred of his mother. It's about his love for her. He's visiting all the places where he remembers the two of them spending time together!"

More connections flowed through her brain as she connected the dots.

"I think I know how he chooses his victims."

"How?" asked Will.

"The girl on the platform, she was playing loud music," she answered. "The tourist couple interrupted him back at the culvert. I'll bet he's having intense memories, almost reliving the experience of being with his mother like a warm blanket. Anyone who interrupts or gets in the way of him getting to that emotional state, is killed!"

"Brilliant, Valerie," Will said.

"But where will he go next?" asked Monaghan.

Valerie took out her phone and looked at the area. "He's moving along a line here. This station isn't far from where his mother was killed, actually. That could very well be his next stop."

"We'll have to be careful," Will said. "He'll be at his most vulnerable and dangerous where his mother was murdered."

"There's no 'we' about it," Valerie said, standing wearily to her feet. "You're getting looked over by a medic and resting, Will."

"I'm fine." But Will tried to stand up and then fell back down onto the bench.

"Don't worry, Doc," said Monaghan. "I'll go with Valerie, if that's okay with you."

"Great," said Valerie. "Do you have a car nearby?"

"Yeah," said Monaghan.

"What about Charlie?" asked Will.

"We've tried to contact him," said Monaghan. "But haven't heard from him yet."

"He's probably in a basement in city hall somewhere," said Valerie. "Still looking for where that culvert comes out. I'll message him about where we're going."

"Take care," Will said, wearily.

Valerie hugged him harder than she ever had before and then rushed off with Monaghan to his car.

She just hoped she could get to the location before Frederick Pitt could claim another victim.

# CHAPTER TWENTY SEVEN

Valerie thought the harbor seemed peaceful, but it had once been the scene of a terrible crime. The murder of Frederick Pitt's mother. She now worried that history was repeating itself, and something just as bad, if not worse, was about to happen there.

Monaghan had driven them there in his own car. An old beat up Chevrolet. Not exactly police issue, but it was as grizzled as Monaghan himself, and somehow that was fitting to Valerie.

They got out and looked at the harbor It was a small marina, filled with yachts and smaller boats.

"It's quiet," Valerie said, feeling the pain of the burns on her arms. She had to get pain killers as soon as they were done.

They walked onto the wooden walkway. It moved between the boats. Their footsteps thudded against it and the water beneath. Valerie saw her reflection in the water.

*I look a mess*, she thought. But then, she'd been through hell. One reflection looked unnervingly like her mother staring back. She couldn't tell if it was her imagination or not, torturing her yet again.

Valerie looked between the masts bobbing up and down in the harbor

"Do you see anything?" asked Monaghan.

"No," said Valerie. "Once some more patrol cars are here, we can get a proper search done. But for now, let's stay on our toes in case he's already here."

Valerie pulled out her revolver. Still wet from the tunnels.

Monaghan pulled out an old magnum.

Valerie smiled. "No pulling your punches then?"

"I don't shoot to incapacitate," he said. "If he's here and he tries anything, I'm putting him down."

They moved off, Monaghan continued: "I still don't get why he's dressed up as homeless. Checking him out, he's got a good apartment, even a decent job, and yet he's down in the tunnels dressed like he hasn't bathed in a year."

"I think it's all about getting closer to his mother," Valerie explained. "He's trying to relive the past times with her. Dressing like he did probably when they were both on the streets. But he also *hates* the homeless in a strange way. And I think I know why."

A scream sounded, cutting through the quiet marina like a pick through ice.

"This way!" Valerie shouted.

They turned down several paths as the walkway continued, until they saw her: A woman. Homeless by the looks of it. She was bleeding from her arm.

"Help!" she shouted.

Monaghan ran, but Valerie realized the danger.

"No, Hank, wait!"

But just as Hank got within touching distance of the woman, the figure of Frederick Pitt appeared from behind a boat. He stuck his knife into Monaghan's chest.

The man didn't even scream. He fell back, pulling the knife from the wound and then collapsing in a heap.

Valerie let off two shots. Both lodged in a boat that Frederick ducked behind. Valerie rushed to Monaghan. She could see that the woman wasn't mortally wounded, though still screaming.

But Monaghan had been stabbed in the chest.

Valerie pulled the woman over to her.

"I'm sorry. I know you're hurt. But put your hands here to stop this man from bleeding out. Help is on the way."

But help had already arrived.

Valerie stood up, watching Frederick trying to escape down the walkway. Suddenly, a tall, powerful figure appeared from the other side, blocking his way.

It was Charlie. His nose was bloodied, Valerie could see the droplets on his shirt as though he had been in a fight or crash.

Frederick looked terrified; he turned back and started running towards Valerie.

She pointed her gun at him: "Stop Frederick. Please. You need help. I can get you it. Just please stop."

"Help!" he shouted. "Where were people like you when my mother died? Where was your help then?"

"I know you've been through a lot," Valerie said. "But we can't let you keep doing this."

"You've got no choice! And neither do I!" he shouted, turning to the water. "You'll never catch me."

146

He stood dazed for a moment as if in thought, and then he turned and started to run towards Valerie.

"Stop!" Valerie yelled. "Stop or I'll shoot!"

But he didn't stop. He was relentless. And he would go on killing unless they nullified him.

"Don't make me do it!" Valerie screamed.

But the man, powerful yet wiry, as though he had been starving himself, continued to run. His feed padded the wooden walkway.

"Out of the way!" Charlie yelled as a couple of bystanders walked between him and the killer without realizing the danger.

Charlie didn't have a clean shot.

Valerie, gave one more warning.

"Frederick, please stop or I'll shoot!"

But nothing would stop him.

Valerie squeezed the trigger. She felt the click she was used to. But nothing happened. The gun had misfired, most probably due to damage or water.

The killer, now only a few feet from her, reached out his arms, his face devilish, showing his gritted teeth.

Valerie tried to fire again, but the gun was done. She readied for the fight of her life, but she could feel it in her bones. Exhaustion. Weariness. She knew she would not be at her best. Would Charlie get to her in time to help before he had turned her into another victim?

The killer leaped towards her violently, wrapping his hands around her throat.

The world slowed down. Valerie could feel the beating of her heart. She thrust her hand into Frederick's chest. But he took the impact and squeezed harder.

In the distance, as Valerie felt the life draining out of her, she saw Charlie trying to get past the bystanders to get to her.

But he was too far away.

Valerie struck at Frederick and tried to pull his hands from her neck. But she was too tired, she'd been through too much. Her body was at its breaking point.

She thought of Tom. She thought of holding his hand. She knew she would never get to do that again. She hated herself for leaving so many things unsaid.

A shot finally sounded.

Frederick Pitt's lifeless body crumpled back onto the wooden walkway before slipping into the water.

Turning, Valerie gasped for air and saw Monaghan sitting up clutching his chest.

"Would someone get me an ambulance," he said groggily, blood oozing out over his hand. "This is my only suit."

The sound of sirens filled the air as Charlie approached.

"You okay?" he asked.

Valerie nodded.

Both of them attended to Monaghan and the injured woman.

"Where were you?" Valerie asked, her voice hoarse.

"I got into an accident…" Charlie said. "Val, I'm going to need to go home right away. Something's come up. Now the case is finished… Where's Will?"

"Feeling better than me," said Monaghan.

Charlie looked at the wound in his chest. "You'll live. It hasn't reached your lungs or heart."

"Well, that's comforting," said Monaghan, sarcastically. "Frederick is dead then?"

"Yeah," said Charlie.

"I think you can put this one behind you now, Monaghan," Valerie said. "We all can."

"I'd say let's celebrate," said Monaghan. "But I think I'm going to be out of it for a while."

"Another time, perhaps," said Valerie, somberly looking at the dead body of the killer.

Police sirens and ambulances soon arrived. The case was closed and Valerie was exhausted. Now, more than anything, she just wanted to go home and pick up where she and Tom had left things.

She had some things she needed to say to him.

# EPILOGUE

Charlie pulled up outside of his home. It was late, but the lights were on. Most likely, Marvin was up regaling his family with made up stories of his heroics, keeping Charlie's kids up well beyond their bedtime.

Stepping out of the car. Charlie breathed in the air. He knew the air around his home. It made him feel at ease. He could banish the worries of his job for a while.

Charlie wearily pulled out his house keys, unlocked the front door and went inside.

"Hey, Honey," he said. "That's me home."

He heard some movement in the dining room. So, he walked down the hallway, opened the door, and expected to see his family up playing a board game or some cards at the table.

Instead, his blood pressure rose up at what he saw.

His kids and wife *were* at the table. Marvin, too. They looked at Charlie with wide, pleading eyes, their mouths covered with tape.

Charlie didn't have much time to react as the masked man behind the door leaped out at him, thrusting a knife at his throat.

\*

"Dad, please," Valerie pleaded.

"No!" he said, standing up in the living room of his house. "You told me you wanted to talk about our relationship as father and daughter, not to get that damned DNA test again!"

"If you don't give this to me," Valerie asked. "How will I ever know the truth about who my biological father is?"

"I am your father. Period."

"Yeah, the only one I've known, Dad," she said angrily. "But you abandoned us."

"I had no choice!" he said, holding his head as if in pain. "Your mother's sickness was getting worse. I wanted to take you with me, but she wouldn't let me. And no one believed me that there was something wrong with her, not until she cut you!"

"And then where were you after that?" Valerie asked.

But he remained silent as if ashamed.

"I'm begging you, please, Dad. It's one swab of your cheek. You never have to hear from me again if you don't want to."

"No," he said.

"I guess that's that, then," Valerie said, her voice becoming cold.

She walked out of the house, slamming the door behind her.

Out front, Tom was waiting in a parked car. Valerie got into the passenger seat.

"You okay?" he asked.

"No," she said. "I didn't even get a chance to tell him about this." She pointed to the engagement ring on her finger. She'd taken to wearing it ever since coming home.

After thinking her friend Will had died for a time, and how close she herself had come to death on the case, she realized life was short. She still wasn't sure how it would work, not if her illness had anything to say about it. But she wanted to be around the people she loved most.

And that was most certainly Tom.

"I did, however," Valerie said, "get this." She pulled a coffee mug out of her pocket.

"Was that his?" Tom said in disbelief.

"Yup. He was drinking from it. I'm sure the lab at work can get his DNA from it, then I can finally find out if he's really my dad or not."

"And then what?" said Tom.

"I don't know," she answered. "I'm making this up as I go along. But if he isn't my real dad, I want to know who is, and what happened to him."

The image of her mother cackling in her psych room jumped into Valerie's mind for a moment. She banished it as best she could. But she could not banish the terrible worry that, if someone else *was* her dad, that her own mother had done something to him.

"Tom," she said quietly. "I've decided to go to a therapist Will recommended. I think it might be good for me to work through some things. Be the best I can be, you know?"

Tom turned and smiled at her. "Whatever you need to do, I support, Val."

Valerie's phone suddenly pinged.

"I hope that's not work," Tom sighed. "I was hoping we could try out that new Mexican place."

Valerie read the text message and instantly felt ill. Something was terribly wrong.

"We have to go to Charlie's house. Now."

# NOW AVAILABLE!

## NO QUARTER
### (A Valerie Law FBI Suspense Thriller—Book 5)

**From #1 bestselling mystery and suspense author Blake Pierce comes book #5 in a gripping new series: former mental hospital patients are being found dead, and the FBI's elite criminally-insane unit is summoned to crack the pattern. The murders bear the signature of a psychotic killer, and Special Agent Valerie Law suspects that entering his mind may just bring her down a darker rabbit hole than she would ever dare to venture...**

"A masterpiece of thriller and mystery."
—Books and Movie Reviews, Roberto Mattos (re *Once Gone*)

NO QUARTER is book #5 in a new series by #1 bestselling mystery and suspense author Blake Pierce.

A page-turning crime thriller featuring a brilliant and haunted new female protagonist, the VALERIE LAW mystery series is packed with suspense and driven by a breakneck pace that will keep you turning pages late into the night. Fans of Rachel Caine, Teresa Driscoll and Robert Dugoni are sure to fall in love.

Book #6 in the series—NO CHANCE—is now also available.

"An edge of your seat thriller in a new series that keeps you turning pages! ...So many twists, turns and red herrings... I can't wait to see what happens next."
—Reader review (*Her Last Wish*)

"A strong, complex story about two FBI agents trying to stop a serial killer. If you want an author to capture your attention and have you guessing, yet trying to put the pieces together, Pierce is your author!"

—Reader review (*Her Last Wish*)

"A typical Blake Pierce twisting, turning, roller coaster ride suspense thriller. Will have you turning the pages to the last sentence of the last chapter!!!"
—Reader review (*City of Prey*)

"Right from the start we have an unusual protagonist that I haven't seen done in this genre before. The action is nonstop... A very atmospheric novel that will keep you turning pages well into the wee hours."
—Reader review (*City of Prey*)

"Everything that I look for in a book... a great plot, interesting characters, and grabs your interest right away. The book moves along at a breakneck pace and stays that way until the end. Now on go I to book two!"
—Reader review (*Girl, Alone*)

"Exciting, heart pounding, edge of your seat book... a must read for mystery and suspense readers!"
—Reader review (*Girl, Alone*)

## Blake Pierce

Blake Pierce is the USA Today bestselling author of the RILEY PAGE mystery series, which includes seventeen books. Blake Pierce is also the author of the MACKENZIE WHITE mystery series, comprising fourteen books; of the AVERY BLACK mystery series, comprising six books; of the KERI LOCKE mystery series, comprising five books; of the MAKING OF RILEY PAIGE mystery series, comprising six books; of the KATE WISE mystery series, comprising seven books; of the CHLOE FINE psychological suspense mystery, comprising six books; of the JESSE HUNT psychological suspense thriller series, comprising twenty four books; of the AU PAIR psychological suspense thriller series, comprising three books; of the ZOE PRIME mystery series, comprising six books; of the ADELE SHARP mystery series, comprising sixteen books, of the EUROPEAN VOYAGE cozy mystery series, comprising four books; of the new LAURA FROST FBI suspense thriller, comprising nine books (and counting); of the new ELLA DARK FBI suspense thriller, comprising eleven books (and counting); of the A YEAR IN EUROPE cozy mystery series, comprising nine books, of the AVA GOLD mystery series, comprising six books (and counting); of the RACHEL GIFT mystery series, comprising eight books (and counting); of the VALERIE LAW mystery series, comprising nine books (and counting); of the PAIGE KING mystery series, comprising six books (and counting); of the MAY MOORE mystery series, comprising six books (and counting); the CORA SHIELDS mystery series, comprising three books (and counting); and the NICKY LYONS FBI suspense thriller series, comprising three books (and counting).

An avid reader and lifelong fan of the mystery and thriller genres, Blake loves to hear from you, so please feel free to visit www.blakepierceauthor.com to learn more and stay in touch.

NO REFUGE (Book #7)
NO GRACE (Book #8)
NO ESCAPE (Book #9)

**RACHEL GIFT MYSTERY SERIES**
HER LAST WISH (Book #1)
HER LAST CHANCE (Book #2)
HER LAST HOPE (Book #3)
HER LAST FEAR (Book #4)
HER LAST CHOICE (Book #5)
HER LAST BREATH (Book #6)
HER LAST MISTAKE (Book #7)
HER LAST DESIRE (Book #8)

**AVA GOLD MYSTERY SERIES**
CITY OF PREY (Book #1)
CITY OF FEAR (Book #2)
CITY OF BONES (Book #3)
CITY OF GHOSTS (Book #4)
CITY OF DEATH (Book #5)
CITY OF VICE (Book #6)

**A YEAR IN EUROPE**
A MURDER IN PARIS (Book #1)
DEATH IN FLORENCE (Book #2)
VENGEANCE IN VIENNA (Book #3)
A FATALITY IN SPAIN (Book #4)

**ELLA DARK FBI SUSPENSE THRILLER**
GIRL, ALONE (Book #1)
GIRL, TAKEN (Book #2)
GIRL, HUNTED (Book #3)
GIRL, SILENCED (Book #4)
GIRL, VANISHED (Book 5)
GIRL ERASED (Book #6)
GIRL, FORSAKEN (Book #7)
GIRL, TRAPPED (Book #8)
GIRL, EXPENDABLE (Book #9)
GIRL, ESCAPED (Book #10)

GIRL, HIS (Book #11)

**LAURA FROST FBI SUSPENSE THRILLER**
ALREADY GONE (Book #1)
ALREADY SEEN (Book #2)
ALREADY TRAPPED (Book #3)
ALREADY MISSING (Book #4)
ALREADY DEAD (Book #5)
ALREADY TAKEN (Book #6)
ALREADY CHOSEN (Book #7)
ALREADY LOST (Book #8)
ALREADY HIS (Book #9)

**EUROPEAN VOYAGE COZY MYSTERY SERIES**
MURDER (AND BAKLAVA) (Book #1)
DEATH (AND APPLE STRUDEL) (Book #2)
CRIME (AND LAGER) (Book #3)
MISFORTUNE (AND GOUDA) (Book #4)
CALAMITY (AND A DANISH) (Book #5)
MAYHEM (AND HERRING) (Book #6)

**ADELE SHARP MYSTERY SERIES**
LEFT TO DIE (Book #1)
LEFT TO RUN (Book #2)
LEFT TO HIDE (Book #3)
LEFT TO KILL (Book #4)
LEFT TO MURDER (Book #5)
LEFT TO ENVY (Book #6)
LEFT TO LAPSE (Book #7)
LEFT TO VANISH (Book #8)
LEFT TO HUNT (Book #9)
LEFT TO FEAR (Book #10)
LEFT TO PREY (Book #11)
LEFT TO LURE (Book #12)
LEFT TO CRAVE (Book #13)
LEFT TO LOATHE (Book #14)
LEFT TO HARM (Book #15)
LEFT TO RUIN (Book #16)

ONCE TRAPPED (Book #13)
ONCE DORMANT (Book #14)
ONCE SHUNNED (Book #15)
ONCE MISSED (Book #16)
ONCE CHOSEN (Book #17)

**MACKENZIE WHITE MYSTERY SERIES**
BEFORE HE KILLS (Book #1)
BEFORE HE SEES (Book #2)
BEFORE HE COVETS (Book #3)
BEFORE HE TAKES (Book #4)
BEFORE HE NEEDS (Book #5)
BEFORE HE FEELS (Book #6)
BEFORE HE SINS (Book #7)
BEFORE HE HUNTS (Book #8)
BEFORE HE PREYS (Book #9)
BEFORE HE LONGS (Book #10)
BEFORE HE LAPSES (Book #11)
BEFORE HE ENVIES (Book #12)
BEFORE HE STALKS (Book #13)
BEFORE HE HARMS (Book #14)

**AVERY BLACK MYSTERY SERIES**
CAUSE TO KILL (Book #1)
CAUSE TO RUN (Book #2)
CAUSE TO HIDE (Book #3)
CAUSE TO FEAR (Book #4)
CAUSE TO SAVE (Book #5)
CAUSE TO DREAD (Book #6)

**KERI LOCKE MYSTERY SERIES**
A TRACE OF DEATH (Book #1)
A TRACE OF MURDER (Book #2)
A TRACE OF VICE (Book #3)
A TRACE OF CRIME (Book #4)
A TRACE OF HOPE (Book #5)

Lightning Source UK Ltd.
Milton Keynes UK
UKHW010253090223
416650UK00002B/397